When C[...]
backward to clear a path. The knife hissed past his stomach, but came back in an even deadlier strike. Clint lowered his left arm and tensed his muscles, fully expecting to feel the sharpened steel cut through his flesh. It did, but only as it was deflected by Clint's block.

Without wasting a single moment that he'd just bought for himself, Clint grabbed the other man's arm to keep it from swinging the blade again. From there, he pounded the knuckles of his free hand into the bones just below the dark-skinned man's wrist. He thought he felt one of the bones snap, but couldn't be sure.

When Clint stepped into him and turned to one side, he managed to catch the incoming knee before it gained any steam. One more hit to the same spot on the other man's arm, followed by a backhand to the mouth, put the fighter out of the brawl.

As if trying to pounce on that very opportunity, Holling shouted, "A hundred dollars to the man who drops that prick!"

DON'T MISS THESE
ALL-ACTION WESTERN SERIES
FROM THE BERKLEY PUBLISHING GROUP

THE GUNSMITH by J. R. Roberts
Clint Adams was a legend among lawmen, outlaws, and ladies. They called him . . . the Gunsmith.

LONGARM by Tabor Evans
The popular long-running series about Deputy U.S. Marshal Long—his life, his loves, his fight for justice.

SLOCUM by Jake Logan
Today's longest-running action Western. John Slocum rides a deadly trail of hot blood and cold steel.

BUSHWHACKERS by B. J. Lanagan
An action-packed series by the creators of Longarm! The rousing adventures of the most brutal gang of cutthroats ever assembled—Quantrill's Raiders.

DIAMONDBACK by Guy Brewer
Dex Yancey is Diamondback, a Southern gentleman turned con man when his brother cheats him out of the family fortune. Ladies love him. Gamblers hate him. But nobody pulls one over on Dex . . .

WILDGUN by Jack Hanson
The blazing adventures of mountain man Will Barlow—from the creators of Longarm!

TEXAS TRACKER by Tom Calhoun
Meet J.T. Law: the most relentless—and dangerous—manhunter in all Texas. Where sheriffs and posses fail, he's the best man to bring in the most vicious outlaws—for a price.

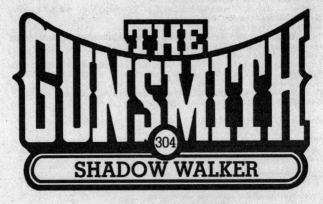

THE GUNSMITH

304

SHADOW WALKER

J. R. ROBERTS

JOVE BOOKS, NEW YORK

THE BERKLEY PUBLISHING GROUP
Published by the Penguin Group
Penguin Group (USA) Inc.
375 Hudson Street, New York, New York 10014, USA
Penguin Group (Canada), 90 Eglinton Avenue East, Suite 700, Toronto, Ontario M4P 2Y3, Canada
(a division of Pearson Penguin Canada Inc.)
Penguin Books Ltd., 80 Strand, London WC2R 0RL, England
Penguin Group Ireland, 25 St. Stephen's Green, Dublin 2, Ireland (a division of Penguin Books Ltd.)
Penguin Group (Australia), 250 Camberwell Road, Camberwell, Victoria 3124, Australia
(a division of Pearson Australia Group Pty. Ltd.)
Penguin Books India Pvt. Ltd., 11 Community Centre, Panchsheel Park, New Delhi—110 017, India
Penguin Group (NZ), 67 Apollo Drive, Mairangi Bay, Auckland 1311, New Zealand
(a division of Pearson New Zealand Ltd.)
Penguin Books (South Africa) (Pty.) Ltd., 24 Sturdee Avenue, Rosebank, Johannesburg 2196,
South Africa

Penguin Books Ltd., Registered Offices: 80 Strand, London WC2R 0RL, England

SHADOW WALKER

A Jove Book / published by arrangement with the author

PRINTING HISTORY
Jove edition / April 2007

ISBN: 978-0-515-14285-3

JOVE®
Jove Books are published by The Berkley Publishing Group,
a division of Penguin Group (USA) Inc.,
375 Hudson Street, New York, New York 10014.
JOVE is a registered trademark of Penguin Group (USA) Inc.
The "J" design is a trademark belonging to Penguin Group (USA) Inc.

PRINTED IN THE UNITED STATES OF AMERICA

10 9 8 7 6 5 4 3 2 1

ONE

Tad's Billiards was the biggest business in town. Of course, for a town the size of Markton, Wyoming, that wasn't saying a whole lot. Apart from earning as much as a few of the stores combined and holding its own against both of Markton's hotels, it was the center of attention on Markton's main street.

The place was two floors high and sported a freshly painted sign that most locals considered garish. That sign didn't mean much to Tad's regular customers, though. All that interested them was what went on inside.

All but one actual billiard table had been hauled away years ago. The one that remained stood by itself in a corner, collecting dust and beer stains as folks took in some of the more popular attractions. One of those attractions was the array of gambling tables scattered throughout the place. Another attraction was the entertainment that moved around the main floor, enticing men to the rooms above.

The working girls came in a wide mix of shapes, sizes, colors and temperament. They dressed in everything from clothes they'd stitched together themselves to fashions that had supposedly come straight from Paris. At any time of day, Tad's was full of noises to hear and sights to see. Most

1

of those sights and sounds were made by drunks stumbling to and from the bar near the front door. Thanks to them, there was no need for a stage show. They were also the reason why the barkeeps, dealers, servers and working girls alike all carried some sort of weapon.

None of this was kept a secret, but none of it discouraged the drunks from raising hell. In fact, some of the nastier drunks took it as a challenge to try and get away with something in Tad's.

Nobody had ever accused drunks of being smart, but some drunks were dumber than others. The only good thing about them was that they were real easy to pick out of a crowd.

"Hot damn! That boy can play the hell out of that fiddle!"

Although the fiddle player was barely plucking out a tune, he nodded a quick thanks to Andy Phillips and looked the other way.

"Maybe you should take it easy there, Andy," one of the men at Phillips's table said.

"To hell with that! I knows me some good music when I hears it and that's some damn fine music right there!"

The two other men at Andy's table chuckled and shook their heads. Both of them were in their early twenties, which made them at least five years younger than Andy. One of the men had a scar on his chin and the other had a chin that looked as if it hadn't even considered sprouting a whisker.

Andy, himself, had a pockmarked face with uneven scrub covering his chin and cheeks. Short, greasy, red hair was plastered against his scalp and still had dust in it from his ride into Markton three days ago. He was a skinny fellow with a face that was always twisted into a scowl. Bony hands were wrapped around a bottle of whiskey, which he continually slammed against the table in time to the beat he thought he was hearing in the music.

"I wanna see some dancin' girls!" Andy demanded. "Bring out the dancin' girls!"

"There's no stage, Andy," the smooth-faced kid said.

"I don't care! I still wanna see some dancin' girls." Andy's eyes widened when he spotted a pretty brunette walking from the ring of nearby faro tables. "Hey now. There's a sight for sore eyes. Come on over here, darlin'."

The girl looked to be as old as the two younger men at Andy's table and she responded instantly to Andy's lecherous gaze. She had a round face, full lips and dark eyes. Her skin was tanned a light brown and looked smooth as silk. The smile she showed to the three men was even smoother.

"Howdy," she said with a hint of a Texas accent. "You fellas look like you're having a good time."

"I sure am," Andy slurred. "You want to dance for me?"

"I can do plenty more than that for five dollars. You can even take me upstairs and have me all to yourself."

Andy's eyes were like dirty panes of glass in front of an empty display case. They were hazy, with nothing whatsoever behind them. "Five dollars? I got more'n that."

"You want to go upstairs?"

"What's yer name, sweet thing?"

"Jill."

"Jill? I'm Jack. You want to climb my hill?"

Andy laughed at his joke almost as much as his two buddies. Although the girl joined in a bit, it was plain to see that she'd laughed at that same joke plenty of other times.

After clearing his throat, Andy straightened up and put on the most serious expression he could manage. "Tell you what I want, darlin'. I want you to hop onto this table here and get to dancin'."

"I don't think Sal would like that too much," she replied.

"Then get Tad out here. I can tell him how much I like his place. I'll bet he wouldn't mind if you danced for us payin' customers."

"Tad?" Jill's eyes widened a bit as she nodded. "Oh, there's no Tad. I think he sold this place way before I started working here."

The man with the scar on his chin burped and muttered, "Just dance, bitch."

Jill scowled and turned to fix an angry glare at the man who'd spoken. Less than a second later, she swiped her hand out and caught him across the face with a loud slap.

The two men flinched as if they'd also been slapped. When they got a good look at their friend's surprised face, they broke out into raucous laughter.

"That might've been worth the five bucks right there!" Andy hollered.

Although the fire in her eyes had died down a bit, Jill wasn't trying to force a smile any longer. "Any of you boys want to have some fun with me, or do you just want to keep it between yourselves?"

"You know what I want, bitch," Andy snarled as the laughter dried up quicker than a puddle in the desert. "But before I pay anything, I'd like to get a sample of the merchandise."

With that, Andy reached out to grab hold of Jill's wrist and pull her closer to him like he was reeling in a fish. When Jill started to squirm and struggle, Andy only grinned up at her.

Andy pushed himself out from his table and forced Jill to sit on his lap. He then wrapped his left arm around her waist while using his right hand to grope her rounded breasts. "Ehh, I like what you got darlin'," Andy rasped into her ear.

Recoiling from the smell of sweat and whiskey coming off of Andy in waves, she started to get up, but was shoved back down again by the man with the scar on his chin.

Pulling her in tightly against him, Andy said, "You're gonna dance for me and I ain't payin' a fucking penny. But first, I might just have a little fun right here and now." He shoved his hand under her skirts.

Before he could get his hand beneath the layers of material Jill wore, Andy felt his arm get pulled away so forcefully that it almost came out of its socket. Before he knew what was happening, Jill was lifted off of him and moved away from the table.

"What in the hell?" Andy groaned as he turned to get a look at who'd interfered with his party.

"Don't those ears of yours work?" Clint Adams asked as he stepped between Jill and Andy. "The lady told you she didn't want to dance."

TWO

Andy was so drunk that he didn't hesitate in getting to his feet and standing toe to toe with Clint. "And who the hell are you s'posed to be? I ain't run afoul of no pimp because I was gonna pay for this bitch to do what I wanted."

"The money's right here," the youngest man at the table added.

Clint nodded and said, "I'm not a pimp."

"Then get the hell away from us."

"I do work here, however," Clint added. "So I get the pleasure of telling you men to leave."

"Tell all you want," Andy growled. "We ain't going nowhere."

When Andy got up, he didn't have to wait long before the other two men joined him. The sound of those chairs being pushed back was enough to catch the attention of a few nearby customers, but not enough to bring the whole place to a halt.

"There's no need for this to get ugly," Clint said. "All you need is some fresh air and some time to sober up. After that, you're more than welcome to come on back. Isn't that right?"

Answering his question was a beefy man with an olive complexion who stood behind the bar as if he'd been planted there. His head was bald and thick layers of skin gathered at the back of his neck. Listening to what Clint had said, he nodded grudgingly.

"See?" Clint asked. "We're all friends here."

"To hell with that. I want that bitch to dance and that ain't askin' fer much. She's gonna dance, or you'll be dancing after I put my boot up yer ass for steppin' in where you ain't wanted."

"That's a whole lot of tough talk. I'm surprised you're not winded."

Clint had figured that would be enough to either back Andy down or push him over the edge. He was right.

Andy grabbed his bottle and took a swing at Clint's face. Clint stepped back to easily dodge the bottle and even slapped the back of Andy's arm to make sure it kept going away from him. As Andy tried to regain his balance, the other two men with him lunged toward Clint with their hands clenched into fists.

Clint wasn't able to get away from the first punch and felt it crack against his jaw. The impact was enough to rattle him a bit, but not enough to do any damage. Clint was able to send a quick punch into the gut of the man with the scar on his chin. His fist drove in deep and forced all the air from the man's lungs.

The youngest man at the table reached for his boot and got hold of the knife that was sheathed there. When Clint saw the glint from the blade in the younger kid's hand, he could have easily made certain that blade wound up in the scarred man's back rather than his own chest. But Clint moved the scarred man in the opposite direction, so he could confront the kid directly.

As soon as he saw Clint focus on him, the kid with the knife hesitated and staggered a step. That was more than enough time for Clint to grab hold of the kid's wrist and twist it in the wrong direction. The kid let out a pained yelp and couldn't drop the knife fast enough.

From there, all Clint needed to do was toss the kid toward the door and boot him in the backside to make sure he kept on going.

Clint pivoted to get a look at the two men who were left. Andy still had his bottle in hand, while his scarred friend was tightening his grip around the backrest of the closest chair.

"Two of us an' one a him," Andy slurred. "I like them odds!" With that, he cocked back his arm and prepared to swing the bottle again.

Clint raised his left arm to block the swing. Although he stopped the bottle before it did any damage, the impact against his forearm sent a jolt of pain all the way up to Clint's shoulder. Keeping his left arm raised, he slid it around the back of Andy's neck so he could draw him into a powerful, right-handed uppercut.

Andy dropped the bottle, let out another wheeze and was shoved toward the door so he could follow in the kid's footsteps.

Hoping he wasn't too late to keep from getting dropped by a chair, Clint turned to get a look at the only man still standing near the table. Sure enough, the man had screwed up enough courage to take his swing. Either that, or he was just too drunk to know any better.

The scarred man let out a visceral growl as he picked up the chair and swung it toward Clint.

Clint could see the scarred man was putting all of his strength behind swinging the chair. That didn't mean he was about to stand there and let himself get hit.

Moving in the same direction as the incoming chair, Clint managed to stay ahead of it until the man swinging it had lost most of its momentum. Now that he was in close to the scarred man, Clint could pick his shot. He decided on a simple uppercut and dropped the scarred man with ease.

Thanks to the liquor in his system, the scarred man was able to scramble onto his feet before he truly felt the pain from getting hit. His eyes were big as saucers as they fixed upon the closest thing on the floor that was within his reach.

Andy's bottle had been chipped in the fall, but was still mostly intact. What made it even more appealing was the fact that the bottom had been broken enough to form a circle of jagged, shattered glass. When he grabbed the neck of the bottle, the scarred man grinned as if he'd already won the fight.

Before he could lift the bottle, however, the scarred man felt something slam down onto the top of his hand like a hunk of rock that had been tossed from on high. Clint's boot caught the man's fingers and smashed the bottle clenched within them.

Glass shattered, driving shards into the floor and the scarred man's hand.

Ignoring the screams and profanities spewing from the man's mouth, Clint pushed away the remains of the bottle and lifted him to his feet. "You see what happens when you're not polite?" he asked.

While making sure the scarred man wasn't carrying any other weapons, Clint took a quick look over his shoulder. He was more than a little surprised to find Andy still standing near the door. But Clint wasn't as surprised to see the gun in Andy's hand.

Clint glanced quickly over to the bar and got a nod from the burly man behind it. Sal might not have been anxious to have his customers gunned down, but he was plenty quick to give the word for Clint to do what was necessary.

The fact of the matter was Clint wasn't asking for permission to draw. He wanted to see if Sal had him covered—but Clint seemed to be on his own.

Suddenly, a shot cracked through the air. Andy staggered back and blood sprayed from his right shoulder.

"Go on and get out of here," Jill said as she stared along the top of the smoking gun in her hand. "Or I won't be so nice with my next shot."

Clint's hand was on the grip of his modified Colt, but he didn't have any reason to draw the pistol.

Spitting out a few whiskey-soaked curses, Andy pitched his gun toward the bar and stormed out.

Now that the show was over, the drunks got back to their drinks, the gamblers got back to their games and everything went back to normal in Tad's Billiards.

THREE

By the time Clint was setting the chairs back into place, a twelve-year-old kid was rushing over to him with a broom and dustpan. Clint stepped back and let the kid do his job as Jill walked over.

"Thanks for helping me out of that," she said.

Clint laughed and replied, "I was just about to say the same thing."

Jill looked down to the gun that was still in her hand. It was smaller than an average pistol, but wasn't just some two-shot derringer, either. Now that she'd given the gun a chance to cool a bit after being fired, she put her leg up on one of the chairs and pulled her skirt aside.

A holster made from cream-colored leather was strapped to her upper thigh. She slipped the gun into its place and waited a few more seconds before slowly easing her skirt back into place. "How about you buy me a drink and we'll be even?"

Since the broken glass had been swept away and the table was now ready for its next customer, Clint sat down and said, "Don't mind if I do."

"The usual?"

"Of course."

Smiling sweetly, Jill walked over to the bar to place the order. Before she could get there, Sal stepped out from behind it with a mug full of beer in each hand, and walked over to Clint's table.

"You should've killed that prick," Sal said as he set the beers down. "Would've done us all a favor."

Clint picked up his mug and took a sip. The brew was thick and tasted as if it had been burnt somewhere along the line, but it went down easily. "Maybe next time," he said. After his second sip, Clint added, "Now I see why you were so ready to give me this job rather than work off the money I owed you."

"A good businessman knows a good thing when he sees it. Having the Gunsmith bust out in my place was worth it just for the bragging rights alone."

"You tell me that game was fixed and I might become real angry," Clint said in a steady tone that sent a chill down Sal's spine.

The burly man was obviously not one to be intimidated, but he did pale a bit when he saw the warning glare in Clint's eye. "No, no," he said quickly. "That's not what I meant."

Clint's steely facade cracked to reveal the mischievous smile underneath it. "I was just fooling. If I can't spot a cheater by now, I deserve to be hung out to dry every now and then. Besides, Lady Luck can't smile on me all the time."

"Nick might have cheated. I never did like the looks of him."

"All Nick did was bluff me like an expert until he caught a full house. It happens." As he leaned back to take another sip and work a kink from his neck, Clint saw a woman accompanying Jill back to his table. "Sometimes, I think I should be thanking you for letting me stay on here."

Watching Jill and other woman slowly work their way toward him, Clint thought this was most definitely one of those times.

The other woman with Jill was slender with straight black hair that hung all the way down to her waist. She wore a bright red dress that was wrapped around her like paper around a present. Shiny threads wove here and there, catching the light inside the place and making it shimmer around her.

Her face was thin and her eyes were shaped in a way that made her look like a treasure from the East. The swagger in her step and the spark in her eyes was anything but demure. In fact, she walked straight up to Clint as if she meant to slap him on the back.

"Well, well," she said. "It seems our new employee is earning his pay."

"Pay?" Clint asked. "I think Sal is holding out on me." Seeing the look on the burly man's face, Clint said, "Still kidding, Sal."

"He's jumpy," the woman in red said as she patted Sal's cheek. "He doesn't like blood spilled on his expensive floors."

"I just don't like trouble in my place," Sal said. "Maybe I should send you packing, Jasmine."

"You can do that if you want to lose all your regular customers."

As much as Sal wanted to fire back another insult, even he couldn't deny the truth in Jasmine's words. Rather than come up with something else, he grumbled, "Your debt still ain't paid off, Adams," and walked away.

Clint shook his head and took another sip of beer.

Jill took a seat on Clint's lap. "The way he grouses, you might think he was the one getting pawed at all day and night."

Clint leaned back, surprised to have the lady in his lap, but he wasn't about to tell her to leave. "Seems like you handled yourself just fine."

"The law around here don't have a problem with men like those three getting what's coming to them," she said.

"But when the damage comes from whores, things usually don't fall in our favor." With that, Jill leaned in and kissed Clint's cheek. "Thank you," she whispered.

Before Clint could say anything in return, Jill gave him a kiss on the mouth that he wouldn't soon forget. Her lips tasted like cherries and her tongue slipped delicately from her mouth to his. A second after the kiss was done, she got up and sauntered over to some other customers who'd been watching her closely.

Clint was left with his mouth open and his lungs empty. "She's good," he said.

"You know there's nothing keeping you here if you want to go," Jasmine told him as she sat in the chair beside him. "You've caught three cardsharps in the last two days, stopped a dozen fights before they got started and run off Lord only knows how many hell-raisers. That's more work than the last half dozen men Sal's hired to do your job."

"You don't know how much I lost."

Jasmine smiled. That, alone, was enough to bring out even more intricacies of her face. Her nose and cheeks looked as if she had some Indian in her bloodline, while her skin tone and mouth seemed vaguely Spanish. Her eyes and coal black hair were traits from the Far East, but her accent was a bit European.

All of that may have seemed like an odd mix when considered separately, but the whole package was anything but bad. Every move Jasmine made was exotic and every word she spoke was laced with promise.

"I heard you were a good gambler," she said.

"Were?"

Shrugging, she explained, "I'd like to see you argue otherwise while you're working to pay off a loan from Sal."

Clint laughed and gave a quick shrug of his own. "It was a hell of a hand. Even good gamblers have their hard times."

Jasmine leaned forward and placed her hand upon

Clint's knee as if to support herself. Letting her fingers drift between his legs, she whispered, "Feels like you're having a hard time right now."

"I thought you were in charge of the girls in here but weren't supposed to get too close with the customers."

"I do whatever I feel like," she said in a whisper that cut through Clint like a warm knife. "And you're not a customer."

Clint finished his beer, set the mug down and then got up. "I guess it's not my place to argue."

Jasmine got up, too, and led Clint by the hand toward the stairs leading to the upper rooms. Nearly every man in the place was watching the shift of Jasmine's hips as she walked by and the little grin on her face meant she knew it.

FOUR

Jasmine's room wasn't set up for entertaining. In fact, no matter how many promises she gave with her eyes or how much torture she inflicted with the movement of her body, the only entertaining she did was in making sure the customers got the girl they wanted and the services they'd paid for.

Her suite was part bedroom and part office, with a four-poster bed in one corner and a rolltop desk in the other. Jasmine led Clint into the room, shut the door and placed her palms flat against his chest, backing him toward the bed.

"Is this for stepping in on Jill's behalf?" Clint asked as he slid his hands up and down along Jasmine's sides.

She thought about it for a second and then shook her head. "No. It's because I've always wanted to."

Clint wrapped his arm around her a little tighter and finally found the clasps which held her dress shut. It took a bit of doing, but he managed to get them loosened without much difficulty. Once the dress came open, Clint slipped his hand underneath it and found Jasmine's skin to be even smoother than the silk she wore.

She leaned her head back and wriggled slightly in Clint's embrace. That subtle bit of motion was enough to loosen her dress even more until it slid down along her body to reveal pert breasts and small, dark nipples. After a few shakes of her head, her hair flowed over both shoulders. The longest ends dangled down just low enough to brush against the uppermost curve of her backside.

Clint ran his hands along the gentle curve of Jasmine's spine, then placed them on her hips and moved them up the length of her body again. He took his time and savored every inch of her figure until his touch made it to the soft firmness of her breasts.

Letting out a slow moan, Jasmine lifted her arms and crossed her wrists above her head as if she were simply stretching her back. The arch of her body caused her breasts to stand out even more, prominently displaying her erect nipples.

"Do you like what you see?" she asked.

"Most definitely."

Keeping her eyes closed and her head tossed back a bit, Jasmine smirked and shifted a bit closer to him. She moved her arms up and over Clint's head as if to make it clear that she wasn't about to let him go. Arching her back even more, Jasmine practically commanded Clint's hands to cup her tight little backside.

One of Clint's hands stayed in place, while the other slid down just far enough to move her dress down over her hips. From there, the garment dropped to the floor in a bundle at her feet. The only thing Jasmine wore beneath that dress was a pair of lacy panties that matched her dress perfectly.

Smiling seductively, Jasmine unbuckled Clint's pants and eased them off of him. As she lowered herself to her knees, Clint unbuttoned his own shirt and tossed it onto the pile of his clothes.

Jasmine's lips wrapped around Clint's penis and slid all the way down to the base of his shaft. As her head bobbed back and forth, she reached up with both hands to scrape her nails against Clint's chest. She was doing such a good job on him that she even felt Clint's legs buckle slightly.

He pulled in a few breaths and steadied himself, rather than make her stop long enough for him to sit down. Jasmine's lips were pressed tightly around him and her tongue was massaging every inch that slid into her mouth. All Clint needed to do was ease his hands around her head so he could get her to speed up or slow down whenever he wanted.

Slowly, Jasmine eased back and started using her hands on him. At that moment, someone knocked on the door. Without missing a beat, she looked over her shoulder and said, "Come in."

Clint wasn't about to dive for cover, but he was also shocked as hell that Jasmine would take a visitor in the middle of what she was doing. His shock turned to a rush of excitement when he saw who walked into the room.

"I see you started without me," Jill said as she hurried inside and shut the door behind her.

"I couldn't wait," Jasmine replied. "Do you mind if she joins us, Clint?"

Before he could answer, Clint saw Jill unbutton her dress and take it off. Beneath it, she wore a white corset, silk panties and the small holster strapped around her leg. Jill never took her eyes off of him as she unbuckled the holster and then slipped out of her panties and corset.

"The more the merrier," Clint said as Jasmine stood up and pressed herself against him. "There's not anyone else coming, is there?"

Jasmine grinned and asked, "Don't you think we'll be enough for you?"

Reaching out to take Jill by the hand and pull her closer, Clint said, "I guess there's only one way to find out."

Jill positioned herself so she was rubbing against Clint's left side while Jasmine rubbed against his right. Both of them traced lines along the front of his body until they were each taking turns stroking his cock and massaging his inner thigh.

Clint traded off kissing each of them as his hands wandered along both of their backs and shoulders. When he felt the back of his legs bump against Jasmine's bed, he cupped their backsides and pulled them along with him as he fell back onto the mattress.

Both women landed in a squirming heap on top of him and quickly adjusted to their own positions. Jill laid across the bottom of the bed so she could take up the job that Jasmine had started earlier. Her black hair swayed as her mouth slid up and down along his rigid cock. Soon, she was even touching herself and moaning as she sucked him.

Jasmine had something else in mind as she stood up on the bed, straddled Clint's head and lowered herself onto his face. Just as her pussy was close enough for him to kiss, she reached down and grabbed his hair so she could let him know exactly what she wanted.

But Clint didn't need any instruction. He gladly began to lick her pussy until Jasmine was letting out a series of loud moans. He knew he was hitting the right spot with his tongue when he saw her bracing herself against the wall and clenching her eyes shut in anticipation of her climax.

The more Jill worked her mouth on him, the more Clint returned the favor with Jasmine. Soon, he was feeling something else. Instead of her wet, soft lips and tongue, he felt his penis sliding into something warm and slick.

Jill was riding him now, positioned so that she was facing the bottom of the bed and her back was bumping against Jasmine's back. In no time at all, both women had found their rhythm and moved together on top of Clint. Every time Jasmine lowered herself onto Clint's mouth, Jill took his cock all the way inside of her.

Clint grabbed hold of Jasmine's hips and held her in place so he could drive her all the way into a powerful orgasm. When Jasmine stopped moving, Jill leaned forward and grabbed Clint's ankles so she could ride him without disturbing the other woman.

Once Jasmine caught her breath, she rolled onto the bed beside Clint so she could watch what was still going on.

Jill looked over her shoulder and saw how things had changed. She then turned around so she was facing Clint. Her body had more curves than Jasmine's, but that only made her a different flavor of some very fine candy. Jill straddled Clint and sat up straight so her breasts could bounce with the combined motion of their bodies.

Clint took her by the hips and began pumping into her harder and harder until she was breathing heavier and heavier. Soon, Jill had to lean forward and wrap her arms around Clint as if she were hanging onto a bucking bronco. All the while, he kept thrusting up into her, burying his cock deeply into her wet pussy.

Feeling her strength wane, Clint rolled Jill onto her back. She spread her legs wide so he could settle in between them. When his erection touched the moist lips of her pussy, she reached down to guide him in.

Clint massaged her legs as he slowly moved in and out of her. His hands moved along her soft stomach before settling over her large, round breasts. With just a bit of coaxing from his fingers, he got her nipples good and hard. After that, Jill smiled and squirmed every time he touched the dark, sensitive flesh.

Lowering himself so he was fully on top of her, Clint kissed her deeply on the mouth as his hands wandered along her back. Jill wrapped her legs around him and groaned softly as Clint's hands found her plump buttocks and held onto them tightly.

Now, their passion took on an urgency as they both got closer to their own climaxes. Jill seemed to be moving in that direction a little quicker, since her cries were getting louder by the second. Soon, her fingers were digging into Clint's back and her entire body was straining against him.

When her orgasm came, she arched her back and drove her head furiously against the pillow beneath her.

Clint could feel her lips tightening around his cock in a rhythm that almost perfectly matched her labored breaths. That sensation was more than enough to drive him over the edge, which Jasmine seemed to instinctually know.

Her hands touched Clint's shoulders and eased him off of Jill's trembling body. "I'm not through with you just yet," Jasmine whispered.

As much as Clint wanted to stay where he was, the sight of Jasmine's naked body crawling on the edge of the bed was enough to coax him away. Jill didn't seem to mind that he was climbing off of her. In fact, she scooted to one side and let her hand drift between her legs as she watched what Clint and Jasmine were doing.

Jasmine stayed on all fours and grabbed hold of the footboard of the bed. She then lowered her chest against the mattress and arched her back so her tight little buttocks were lifted up high.

That was all Clint needed to see before he moved in behind her and grabbed her hips. His cock was hard as rock and every muscle of his body ached for release. When he glided into Jasmine from behind, he thought he might explode right then and there.

After making it through that initial moment, Clint grabbed a fistful of Jasmine's hair and pulled her head back as he drove all the way inside of her. Judging by the moan that escaped Jasmine's lips, it wouldn't be long before she exploded again herself.

FIVE

It had been a long time since Clint had slept so soundly. In fact, even when he was finally roused from his sleep, he felt like he wouldn't be able to move for another couple of hours. But the faint sound of a woman crying soon jolted him wide awake.

"What's that?" he asked.

Jill was already up and pulling her clothes on while Jasmine sat up and gathered the sheets over herself.

"I'll go check on it," Jill said.

Clint swung his legs over the side of the bed. "You want me to come along?"

"No, that's all right. You stay here and I'll be right back." Although she wasn't made up as well as when she'd arrived, Jill was covered up enough to step outside. She opened the door and was gone before Clint could insist on joining her.

"Relax," Jasmine said as she laid a hand on his shoulder. "She probably wouldn't want to talk to you anyway."

"Who?"

"Whoever is crying," Jasmine replied. She leaned over to the table next to the bed and found a small case of cigarettes. Taking one and placing it between her lips, she then offered the case to Clint.

"No, thanks," he said.

Jasmine shrugged, grabbed a box of matches from the same table and lit her cigarette.

"Shouldn't you be a little more concerned?" Clint asked. "What if one of your girls is in trouble?"

"Usually, at least one of them is in trouble. If they were the kind of girls to lead steady lives, most of them wouldn't exactly pick this as their first job."

"What if one of them is up against someone out to hurt them?"

"It's not that sort of trouble," Jasmine replied confidently.

"How do you know?"

"Because," she replied while the end of her cigarette flared up, "there weren't any gunshots."

Normally, Clint might have asked if that was enough for them to let Jill handle the problem on her own. But, since he'd been working there for a bit himself, he knew Jasmine's confidence was well founded.

As if picking up on his misgivings, Jasmine explained, "The girls I employ are here of their own accord. I make sure they're well paid, have a roof over their heads and food in their bellies. I make sure they can handle themselves and if they can't, there's someone like you to step in for them. If there's a problem, I'll know about it soon enough."

For the next few minutes, Clint sat on the edge of the bed listening to the crying fade away. It eventually died off completely and was replaced by the normal ruckus that filled Tad's Billiards. When he looked back to Jasmine, he saw her finishing up her cigarette.

"You see?" she said. "I told you so. A few new girls have come in and one of them probably just misses her family."

"What will happen if that's the case?"

"She'll go to them or send them a letter. I don't know. What would you do in that case?"

Clint shrugged and swung his feet back up onto the bed. When Jasmine crawled on top of him, she crossed her arms on his chest and rested her chin against them.

"You're not used to being around so many women who can handle themselves," she teased. "And here I thought you were different from the rest of these cowboys."

"Maybe I just don't like hearing women cry," Clint pointed out.

Jasmine smiled warmly and ran the edge of her finger against his chin. "Then you really are different from most of these assholes. But I already knew that."

Just as Jasmine was leaning in to kiss Clint, she was interrupted by a frantic knock on the door.

"Come in," she said.

The door was pushed open and Jill came rushing into the room. "It's Kaylee. She's down the hall."

"Kaylee? Doesn't she work over on Third Street?"

"Yes, but she came here. She says she needs to hide."

"From what?" Jasmine asked.

"I don't know." Looking to Clint, she asked, "Do you think you could talk to her?"

Clint was already dressed and buckling on his holster.

SIX

Jill knocked on the door that was down the hall from Jasmine's. Rather than wait for an answer, she opened it a bit and peeked inside. "I brought someone to make sure nothing will happen to you. He's the one you heard about."

After a few muffled words from inside, Jill nodded and looked over to Clint. "I really appreciate this."

"She's heard about me?" Clint asked.

Jill shrugged and nodded. "It's not a big town, you know."

Although Clint was no stranger to having folks know about his comings and goings, he didn't know that also applied to when he was chasing off drunks from a gambling hall. Rather than wonder too much about that, he stepped into the room as soon as Jill opened the door for him.

The room was easily half the size of Jasmine's. In fact, it might have been less than half that size, but it was still large enough to accommodate a bed and a few pieces of furniture. It wasn't much, but the girl huddled on the bed looked as if she would have been fine if she were locked in a closet.

The girl looked to be in her late teens or possibly early twenties. She was small enough that it was hard to distin-

guish which. Her black hair fell in tight curls that didn't
even make it to shoulder length. Her wide, brown eyes
stared at Clint and she clutched her arms a bit tighter
around her bent knees.

"Are you Kaylee?" Clint asked.

The girl nodded.

"My name's Clint. What's the matter?"

"You're the one who's been chasing all the men out of
here?"

"I guess you could say that."

She forced a smile onto her face. "I work at the Cherry
Blossom on Third Street. That's where some of the men go
once they can't get in here anymore." Saying that was
enough to dim her smile.

Clint hadn't heard about the Cherry Blossom until after
his bad turn at poker. In fact, he hadn't even heard about it
until his second day working for Sal. Since he didn't have
much cause to visit a cathouse, that wasn't too surprising.
Even if he did need to pay for a woman's company, he
doubted he would have gone to a place like the Cherry
Blossom. By all accounts, it was a rundown place owned
by a man who robbed his own customers if they didn't
spend enough money on his girls.

"Did one of them hurt you?" Clint asked.

Kaylee's eyes slowly wandered away from him and she
shook her head. "No."

"Then what about the man who runs that place? Did he
hurt you?"

"No."

Clint looked over to Jill for some help, but didn't get
anything more than a confused shrug. Hunkering down so
he could look straight into her eyes, he placed his hand on
the side of her face and asked, "Then what's the matter?"

It took a few seconds, but Kaylee finally replied, "My
sister. She's gone."

"Gone?"

"Where'd she go, Kaylee?" Jill asked.

"I . . . don't know. She's just . . . gone. I think they came for her."

Clint didn't like the sound of that one bit. That much must have shown in his voice, because both women in the room cringed when he snarled, "Who are they? Tell me."

Still looking rattled, Kaylee began to explain: "We've heard about other girls who've gone missing, but we thought it was a lot of talk."

Jill saw the disbelief on Clint's face, so she quickly interjected, "Plenty of men who have a lot of working girls under their roof tell stories like that."

"Like what?" Clint asked.

"Like someone will take them away or cut them up if they're on their own. It keeps the girls scared so they don't take off on their own. Most of the younger ones don't know any better than to believe it."

"But this weren't no story," Kaylee said. "We thought it was, but it's not. It's true and now my sister's gone."

"When's the last time you saw her?" Clint asked. Now that he'd taken a breath and calmed down a bit, his voice wasn't as harsh as it had been before.

Kaylee responded to him immediately and some of the panic in her eyes faded away. "I saw her two Sundays ago. We go to church together."

"What about this past Sunday? Did you see her then?"

"No, sir. That's when I started looking around for her."

"You can call me Clint," he told her while patting her hand and then easing back into a chair next to the bed.

That seemed to relax Kaylee even more. She released her grip on her knees and even stretched out her legs so she could straighten her skirts over them. "Sometimes she misses church, but not that often. When she does, it's usually because she's in trouble or . . . working. Either way, I usually track her down and give her hell for it. Sometimes, she has to do the same for me, too."

"That's what sisters are for," Clint said.

Kaylee nodded. "I don't have to go far to find her most times. I couldn't find her for a while, but Mr. Holling said she was just busy every time I asked."

"Both of you work at the Cherry Blossom?" Clint asked.

"I clean up there every now and then. My sister works at the Blossom, but she doesn't want me to spend much time there. I barely get to see her at all anymore."

"What's your sister's name?"

"Alicia."

Since saying her name was almost enough to close Kaylee up again, Clint decided to keep from asking about anything more personal than the facts he needed to know about Alicia. Otherwise, he might have his hands full just trying to get Kaylee calmed down again.

"So you think Holling said Alicia was busy to get you to stop asking questions about her?" Clint asked.

Kaylee nodded. "He told me them things about how he protects his girls and that he'd protect me, too, if I came to work for him like the rest of the girls there do. He said he wouldn't never let anything happen to my sister and that she was fine. When Alicia missed a Sunday mass, I knew something was wrong."

Reluctantly, Clint pointed out, "Today is Wednesday. Have you been looking for her this whole time?"

Kaylee shook her head. "I asked Mr. Holling yesterday, but he said she went to Cheyenne to work at a big saloon there where she could make a hundred dollars or more in no time at all. I went to the room she rents and took a look for myself."

Even though tears were coming to her eyes, Kaylee kept talking and Clint wasn't about to stop her.

"The man who runs the boardinghouse let me into her room because he knew I was her sister. Everything she owned was thrown all over the place. All of the tables and chairs were knocked over. All of her things were tossed around, but there was also her clothes."

"Her clothes were messed up?" Jill asked sympathetically.

"No," Clint said. "Her clothes were still there."

"Yes," Kaylee said quickly. "That's how I knew she didn't go nowhere like Cheyenne or anywhere else. She didn't even pack her coat or bonnet."

"Maybe I should take a look over there for myself," Clint said.

SEVEN

Kaylee told Clint which boardinghouse her sister had lived in and which room was hers. He didn't have to ask her twice to stay behind, but Jill was a harder one to convince.

"Holling is a pig and a bastard to women," she'd said in the hallway outside of the room where Kaylee was huddled. "If he's done something terrible to that poor girl's sister, I want to know about it."

"If he did do something to her, you might be in danger around him as well," Clint pointed out. "And if he didn't, you'd just be wasting your time."

Jill crossed her arms and cocked her head as if she were about to scold Clint for leaving the barn door open. "Do you really think that girl's so worked up over some kind of misunderstanding?"

"I couldn't say yet. That's why I need to get a look for myself."

"Let me come along. I know Holling and I can tell you if he's up to something or maybe even lying to you."

"And you're already dead set on the notion that he's guilty as sin," Clint pointed out. "That's not exactly going to be of much help."

Although Jill began to say something in her own defense, she couldn't come up with much of anything.

Before she tried again, Clint said, "I've done my share of reading people and getting them to talk."

"Yeah. That's how you knew to borrow money to cover a bet that you would lose."

"If you know someone better suited for the job, be my guest. We might even try our luck with the law, if you'd rather."

It was no gamble that Jill wouldn't want to bother with the law. All of the working girls in town knew that no man wearing a badge would show them much of any sympathy.

"I just want to help, that's all," Jill finally told him.

"Then stay here with Kaylee and make sure she doesn't move from this spot until I come back. The last thing we need is for her to go running off to do something foolish. Besides, I think she'd rather not be alone right now."

"You're right. Are you sure there's nothing I can do?"

"Yes. If things go bad, I can handle myself."

"And what if you find out that Kaylee was right and that her sister was taken somewhere?"

"Then I'll think of something else," Clint said. "Now do you want me to get started on this or stand about talking to you some more?"

Jill's answer to that was a roll of her eyes as she stepped to one side until her back bumped against the wall.

Clint walked down the hall and saw Jasmine open her door as he approached it.

"What's all the commotion?" she asked.

"Ask Jill. I'll be right back."

Jasmine obviously had plenty more she wanted to ask, but wasn't about to stand in Clint's way. Seeing as how he was headed down the stairs like an engine that had already gathered a head of steam, it was doubtful she could have stopped him even if she'd wanted to.

•   •   •

The boardinghouse was almost halfway between Tad's and the Cherry Blossom a few streets away. It was a narrow building wedged between a dentist's office and a vacant structure that looked to have once been a bakery. Clint walked in to find himself inside a room that looked like a cross between a hotel lobby and someone's sitting room.

"What can I do fer ya?" a potbellied old man asked as he struggled to get up from his rocker.

"I'd like to get a look inside room number four," Clint said.

The old man grimaced. "You'll want to come back later. It's still kind of a mess, but I do have another room available."

"Actually, I'm here to see the mess."

"Pardon me?"

"I'm a friend of Kaylee's and Alicia's," Clint told him, hoping that would be enough to make an impression.

The old man stared at Clint for a few slack-jawed moments before shrugging and waddling over to a row of keys hanging from hooks in the wall. "Suit yerself, but if you try to steal any of that lady's belongings, I'll call the marshal."

Following the old man to the room, Clint tried to look for anything that struck him as peculiar. Sometimes, it was the smallest thing that rang a bell in his head. Clint didn't always even know the importance of something the first time he saw it. This time, just like any other time he was trying to pick up on a trail, he simply kept his eyes and ears open and hoped for the best.

The old man stepped up to the door of room number four, which didn't look any different than the three other doors before it. After twisting the key in the lock, he shoved it open and swept his arm as if he were the keeper of the Pearly Gates.

"There you go," he muttered. "I'll stay right here, watchin' you."

Clint took one step inside and was instantly reminded of Kaylee's description of what she'd found. True to her story, the room looked as if it had been picked up, shaken and then dropped back down again. "Is this the way you found it?" he asked.

"I'm not in the habit of sifting through other people's things. And since I don't know you from Adam, I'm not letting you go any farther inside. You see she ain't in there and you see how the room was left, so there's no other reason for you to be here."

Since the room was small enough for Clint to see it all from the doorway, there wasn't much need for him to push his way in any farther. From where he was, he could see the toppled furniture and clothes dumped next to the bed. He took a look at the door itself and then asked, "Has anyone else been here asking for her?"

"Not since her sister and them two fellas."

"What two fellas?"

"Some tall fella and an Injun. They were expected."

EIGHT

It was getting late by the time Clint made it over to the Cherry Blossom. Compared to the other saloons on Third Street, the Blossom was one of the nicer ones. Then again, Third Street was known to be a row of filthy storefronts favored by rats and drunks.

The Blossom was a short, wide building that had obviously started off as two smaller ones. Its roof was taller on one side than on the other and had two crooked doors leading inside that were separated by a pane of dirty glass.

Clint walked inside and was immediately recognized by most of the working girls as well as a few of the men standing watch by the door. Since they were more interested in guarding the cash register than anything else, only one of those men left their post to make their way to a bald man sitting at a table in the back.

The bald man practically jumped from his chair and glared across the room at Clint. After swapping a few quick words with the guard, he pulled his suspenders back over his shoulders from where they'd been dangling from his pants and plastered on a filthy smile.

"Well, well, I see the big man from the billiard hall has finally come to see his competition."

Clint shrugged at the bald man and replied, "I never received an invitation, so I didn't think there was any problem."

"No problem. I've just heard a lot about you."

"If you're Holling, then I've heard some things about you, too."

Even though Clint knew well enough the bald man was Holling, pretending that he wasn't sure was a good way to throw Holling off his stride. The comment had an even bigger effect, since the bald man actually seemed perplexed that his legend might not have been as far-reaching as he'd thought.

"What have you heard, Adams? Of course, I doubt I can match up to a big, bad gunfighter like yourself. Sal must think his whores have gold-plated pussies if he needs to hire a killer like you for his henhouse."

"I didn't come here to fight," Clint said in a friendly manner. Putting a not-so-friendly edge in his voice, he added, "I know for a fact you wouldn't want that."

Holling paused and then rekindled his smile. "Fair enough. I'm just a businessman and not the violent sort. What brings you here, Adams?"

"I'd like to have a word with one of the girls who works for you. Her name's Alicia."

"She's the one with that cute little sister, ain't she?"

"Kaylee."

"That's the one. I could sure do some good business if they both—"

"What about Alicia?" Clint interrupted before he gave in and punched Holling in the mouth. "Is she around?"

"Nope. Not for a while."

"What about Kaylee?"

"Come to think of it, she was asking some questions not too long ago. Seemed awfully upset. Can I get you a drink, Adams?"

Clint shrugged. "Why not?"

That brought another grin to Holling's face as he

snapped his fingers at a disinterested barkeep. "Two whiskeys. Just bring 'em over to my table. Come on with me, Adams. Take a load off."

Holling led the way to the table where he'd been sitting before and pulled another chair over. "You could make some real good money working here instead'a that shit-hole billiard parlor."

"Tad's is a nice place," Clint said. Since Holling didn't seem to know about his arrangement with Sal, Clint decided not to correct him. "Besides, I've heard some bad things about what goes on in here."

"You talking about that whore and her sister again?"

"I didn't say I was, but you must have something to say on the subject."

At that moment, the barkeep walked over to deliver the two glasses of whiskey. Holling leaned back as if he were about to get a shave as the barkeep plunked down the glasses and sauntered away. All the while, the wheels in Holling's head were grinding so hard that Clint could all but hear them.

After all of that furious contemplation, the best Holling could come up with was, "I'll tell you the same thing I told Alicia's sister, which is I don't know nothing. Whores aren't exactly reliable. They come and go as they please."

"As they please, huh?"

"There's more than enough women lookin' to sell what they got. I don't need to force any of them into it."

"You're getting awfully upset. Is this a touchy subject?"

"No," Holling grunted. "I just don't like being accused of nothing."

"I didn't accuse you of anything."

Holling's eyes shifted back and forth in their sockets as he downed half of his whiskey.

Clint kept his eyes on Holling until he could see the other man squirm. When the time was right, he asked, "What happened to Alicia?"

"How should I know?"

"Because you stand to lose money if she goes missing. I've seen folks who've lost dogs and been more concerned about it than you are. You must have either been the one to make her disappear or you already covered your losses somehow."

"I told you, I don't control when my girls come and go."

"Then who'd you get to replace her? Where did she go? Was she in any trouble? Any businessman would know something about why he's losing one of his workers. If you take me for a fool . . ."

Holling reacted quickly and held up his hand. "I didn't say any such thing. All I know is that someone busted into her room and might have took off with her."

"When was this?"

"I don't know. A week ago, maybe. She went home and didn't show up again. That's it. I went to check on her myself, and it looked like a goddamn twister went through her room. Whores like her keep all their money socked away like mice, so she probably got robbed. I feel sorry for her, as a matter of fact."

"Then why not mention this earlier?" Clint asked.

"Because there ain't nothing I can do. There ain't nothing anyone can do. She's gone and that's that. Talking about it and going on like this will only make things worse."

"Or draw attention to where it's not wanted?"

When he heard that, Holling twitched. It wasn't much, but it was more than enough to tell Clint he'd struck gold.

Like any animal that had been backed into a corner, Holling could either squirm away or bite. Since squirming hadn't gotten him anywhere so far, he bared his teeth. "I've been polite until now, Adams. I've given you a drink and some of my time. If you've got something to tell me as far as this missing whore is concerned, you'd best say it. Otherwise, get the hell out of my place."

Clint nodded slowly and read everything he could on

Holling's face. He looked around and was also able to read the faces of no less than three of Holling's men. The men were positioned all around Clint and had their hands on the grips of their guns. Although the men seemed a bit nervous, they also looked ready to make a move.

Setting down his drink without having tasted a drop of the whiskey, Clint walked straight past Holling's gunmen and left the Cherry Blossom.

NINE

When Clint approached the marshal's office, he saw a familiar figure stepping out the front door and pulling in a breath of cool, night air. The man was of average height and had broad shoulders. His hat was in hand at the moment, displaying a full head of dark blond hair. When he saw Clint crossing the street, he put his hat on and nodded before heading in the other direction.

"Can I have a word with you, Marshal?" Clint asked.

Marshal Rand stopped, sighed and turned around as if it required a great amount of effort. "You can talk to one of my deputies, if you like. I was just on my way home."

"This will just take a moment. I don't know if you recall, but I'm Clint Adams."

"I know who you are. You're working over at Tad's."

"Only temporarily."

"Not temporary enough, as far as I'm concerned."

Clint would have taken some offense from that if he hadn't already gone down that road when he first agreed to work off his debt to Sal. Marshal Rand had come around, spouting off about how he didn't like saloon owners and pimps hiring gunmen to back them up. He'd left it at a warning since then, mostly because Clint hadn't done anything that would have crossed anyone's line. Even so, that didn't keep the sour look off of the lawman's face.

"Have you heard about the woman who's gone missing?" Clint asked.

Rand scowled and hung his head as it became clear he wouldn't be able to push Clint aside and keep walking home. "What missing girl?"

"Alicia Higgins. She used to work over at the Cherry Blossom."

"Oh, yeah. Her sister's been grousing about something along those lines. What of it?"

"She's still missing, that's what."

"She's a whore," Rand stated. "Whores go missing. They get killed. They get hurt. Maybe if they chose a more respectable profession, they wouldn't have such problems."

"You don't care if she might have been kidnapped or killed?" Clint asked.

"Frankly, they're lucky I tolerate them being in this town at all. They lay down, spread their legs, steal men's money and expect to be protected like they were upright citizens."

"So whores are just fair game in this town?"

"I've got better things to do than look after them. Besides, that's what men like you are paid to do."

"I'm not talking about some woman who got beat up while trying to rob a drunk," Clint said. "I'm talking about a woman who is missing. She's got a family that misses her and hasn't hurt anyone, so there's no reason she should just be forgotten."

"I'll look into it. Now, if you'll excuse me."

When Marshal Rand tried to step around him, Clint sidestepped so that he remained in front of the lawman. Although Rand looked more than a little annoyed by that, Clint spoke quickly to explain himself.

"I think the owner of the Cherry Blossom's got something to do with this girl's disappearance," Clint said.

"He's covering up what he knows and lying about several things that have to do with what happened."

"You've got proof of this?"

"Holling's story is that someone busted into Alicia's room and robbed her. I've been to her room and it was a mess, but nobody busted into it. There were even a few bits and pieces of jewelry scattered around, which is exactly what a robber would be looking for."

"That doesn't prove she was killed or kidnapped."

"Maybe not, but it proves there's something being covered up. If she was killed, then her murderer shouldn't just be able to walk away without a care in the world. And if she was kidnapped, her life may depend on someone giving a damn and coming after her."

"You want to go after her?" Rand growled. "Be my guest. I made it perfectly clear to the owners of every saloon in this town that I wouldn't waste my time chasing down drunks and wild whores. That's why there's only a few such places here.

"That's also why saloon owners hire their own security. If that security gets out of line, I come down on them like the hand of God. It's a fine system and it's worked for years. Unless you can show me some decent folks getting hurt, then you'll just have to step aside before I get cross."

"And what if I decide to look a little deeper?" Clint asked. "It may not sit well with Holling."

"Pimps, whores, card cheats—they're all the same sort of filth in my book. Dig as deep as you want and come to me if you find something worth my time. Otherwise, don't start anything to hurt any good folks or I'll run you out of Markton just like I would anyone else."

Clint smiled and stepped aside. "That's all I wanted to know."

TEN

When Clint returned to the Cherry Blossom, he pushed open the door and glanced around until he spotted the faces of the hired guns that had been there before. He picked out every last one of them and even spotted a few more who might be a problem.

One of the men was a large fellow with dark red hair. The sleeves of his shirt were rolled up to display a set of thickly muscled arms. The moment he saw Clint standing in the doorway, he got up from his stool and stomped over to him.

"Mr. Holling's busy," the redhead grunted. "Go back to Tad's where you belong."

"Find Mr. Holling," Clint said. "I want to talk to him."

The redhead took another step forward and slapped his hand flat against Clint's chest. Although he meant to shove Clint out the door, he only managed to knock him back half a step. "You heard what I said," he said angrily. "Now get the hell out of—"

Clint cut him short by grabbing the redhead's wrist and twisting it hard enough to drop the big man to his knees. While leaning in to apply a bit more pressure, Clint said, "Tell me where Holling is."

"In the back!" the redhead said through the pain flooding from his arm and coursing through his shoulder. "Same table . . . as always!"

"Thanks." Letting go of the redhead's wrist, Clint began walking through the room as if there weren't a thing or person that could stop him.

The Cherry Blossom wasn't empty, but most of its customers were busy in one of the smaller bedrooms in the back. That left only a handful of drunks and a few card players, who were more than willing to step aside and let Clint go wherever the hell he wanted.

Clint could see Holling at the table where he'd been before. The only reason he hadn't seen him right away was because of the two burly men who stood between that table and the front door. One of them had dark skin and cautious eyes, while the other was pale and spoke in a loud, grating voice.

"You ain't wanted here, Adams!" the pale man said. "You were warned, so get out before we call the marshal."

"Already been to see the marshal," Clint said. "He doesn't care about me any more than he does about you."

Standing up and clamoring for his men's attention, Holling shouted, "Just remove him from here, goddamn it!"

That was all the pale man needed to hear and he moved forward while balling up both fists. He lashed out with a quick punch that caught Clint off his guard. His knuckles cracked against Clint's jaw, but didn't do much damage. Going by the look on the pale man's face, one might have thought he'd won a prize.

"You ain't nothing, Adams," the pale man growled. From there, he intended on following up his first punch with another to Clint's nose. He managed to get his arm cocked back before Clint buried his fist in his gut. The pale male doubled over and hacked up a long, strained breath.

Clint turned toward the dark-skinned man, but knew the pale man wasn't done. Without looking at the man he'd just punched, Clint brought up his knee to slam into the pale man's face. That dropped him like a sack of rocks, allowing Clint to deal with his next opponent.

The dark-skinned man must have known who he was dealing with, because his hand faltered when he started to go for the gun holstered at his side. Rather than draw the pistol, he went for the knife strapped to his belt.

When Clint saw the blade slice through the air, he lunged backward to clear a path. The knife hissed past his stomach, but came back in an even deadlier strike. Clint lowered his left arm and tensed his muscles, fully expecting to feel the sharpened steel cut through his flesh. It did, but only as it was deflected by Clint's block.

Without wasting a single moment that he'd just bought for himself, Clint grabbed the other man's arm to keep it from swinging the blade again. From there, he pounded the knuckles of his free hand into the bones just below the dark-skinned man's wrist. He thought he felt one of the bones snap, but couldn't be sure.

The dark-skinned man let out a pained grunt, but somehow held onto his knife. Perhaps taking a note from Clint, he brought up his knee to strike at Clint's ribs.

When Clint stepped into him and turned to one side, he managed to catch the incoming knee before it gained any steam. One more hit to the same spot on the other man's arm, followed by a backhand to the mouth, put the dark-skinned fighter out of the brawl.

Blood seeped into Clint's shirtsleeve and he tapped the fresh wound to get a feel for how bad it was. Despite the blood, he could tell the cut was too shallow to worry about. Therefore, he could pay attention to what mattered before one of Holling's men snuck in a lucky shot.

As if trying to pounce on that very opportunity, Holling shouted, "A hundred dollars to the man who drops that prick!"

None of the customers were interested and the two

guards closest to Holling's table were still trying to catch their breath.

Clint saw the redhead from the corner of his eye and immediately shifted his focus toward the door.

By that time, the redhead was staring intently back at Clint. His hand was wrapped around the grip of his pistol and was already bringing the weapon out from its holster.

Clint saw the gun in the redhead's hand a fraction of a second before his modified Colt cleared leather. Holding the pistol at arm's length, Clint sighted down the barrel and waited.

It didn't take long before the redhead came to his senses. Of course, lowering his gun was an easy choice to make since it hadn't even left its holster.

"All right, all right," Holling said as if he were doing Clint a favor. "That's enough. Come on over here and we can talk."

"If you set me up for another ambush," Clint warned, "I'll be sure to kill you first."

"Don't be silly," Holling sputtered as he motioned Clint toward an empty chair. The next thing he did was wave toward the barkeep, who put away the shotgun he'd been holding.

ELEVEN

Holling was sweating profusely as he sat and waited for Clint to take the seat he'd been offered. Pausing in the middle of reaching for his shirt pocket, he waited for Clint to nod before removing the handkerchief that had been stuffed there.

"Awfully warm tonight," Holling said as he dabbed the sweat from his brow. "What's on your mind, Adams? Or should I call you Clint?"

"Adams is fine," was Clint's icy reply.

"Oh, certainly. Of course."

"First of all, I know you lied to me the last time I was in here," Clint told him.

"Why do you think that?"

"About someone breaking into Alicia's room? The door was in fine shape. Nobody broke into anything."

"The owner could have fixed it," Holling said quickly.

"The owner was too lazy to notice she was even missing."

Holling shrugged a few times, but that wasn't enough to convince Clint. "It's like you said before. I'm the one losing money here."

"Perhaps." Clint settled back into his chair, but didn't let

46

the intensity in his eyes falter in the slightest. "How much did the Indian pay you?"

"W-what?"

"The Indian," Clint repeated. "You know . . . the one who traveled with that tall fellow?"

Holling didn't move. In fact, he kept so still that he looked almost unnatural. The longer he stayed that way, the more it seemed he wanted to crawl under the table and hide. When Holling let out his breath and swallowed another, the knot in his stomach was almost big enough for Clint to see.

"Th-those two aren't . . . I mean . . . I never met those two until a few weeks ago."

Even though he knew he had to maintain the appearance that he knew exactly where the conversation was going, Clint still had to fight awfully hard to keep from smiling. "Go on."

Sensing that his battle had just been lost, Holling let out a breath that seemed to empty his lungs completely. In fact, it even seemed to empty the rest of his body and leave nothing but a shriveled husk. Slouching forward, Holling closed his eyes and pressed his fingers to them. "I didn't even have a damn choice, you know. That asshole Coltraine came in saying he was gonna kill all my girls if I didn't give him at least one."

"He'd kill all the women working here?" Clint asked in disbelief.

"Yeah! Can you believe it? Deplete all my stock just to prove a point! And from the things I've heard about him, he'd do it."

It took all of Clint's strength to keep from knocking Holling out of his boots when he heard the man refer to women as stock. He didn't try too hard to cover up the distaste he felt, since the gleam in his eyes was doing wonders to loosen Holling's tongue.

"Alicia'd been giving me grief for a while," Holling said. "All this talk about wanting me to hire her sister for odd jobs, but not try to get even more money out of her. It's like she owned this place or something."

"Who's Coltraine?"

"He's a bad piece of work. I know some fellas in Wichita who lost every damn one of their whores to him. The ones that didn't come along easy were cut up and booted out in the middle of nowhere. By the time he came around again, the others were more than willing to deal with him."

"Why not stand up to him?" Clint asked. "Surely this can't be the first time anyone tried to hone in on someone else's territory."

"Coltraine's the worst kind of killer. And even if a man could afford the sort of gunman it would take to go against him, there's still the Indians to deal with."

Clint gritted his teeth and looked around the room. Although the guards were pulling themselves together and settling into their positions, they weren't ready to make another move yet. Sensing that situation could change at any moment, Clint put a bit of impatience into his voice when he asked, "Why does Coltraine take the women?"

"Hell if I know. I never sat down to chat with the man."

"Where does he take them?"

"I don't know for certain, but the Injun with him was Crow. They rode toward the north nearly every time they left town, so you can add them numbers together."

"You're sure he was Crow?"

"Yeah. I seen more'n my share when I was a trapper."

"All right, then. Now that we seem to be getting along so well, why don't we take our friendship to new heights?"

Holling scowled suspiciously at Clint and then looked around as if someone were playing a trick on him. Finally, he asked, "What's that supposed to mean?"

"It means that I want to find this Coltraine and you could only benefit if I do. In fact, several men in your line of work in this area could probably benefit if I tracked that man down. If what you say is true, I'll be putting him straight out of business."

Slowly, Holling's face shifted from suspicion to elation. "If someone like yourself couldn't do it, no one could. The law sure don't seem to give a damn."

"And I won't even need any of your men to help me," Clint added.

Holling's eyes narrowed and he asked, "So what do you need?"

"All I need is for you to forget about this meeting in case anyone comes around asking about it." Letting the friendly smile drop right off his face, Clint added, "If you set up an ambush just to prove yourself to your boys, I'll come for you as soon as I'm done with them. If you get angry and decide to smack around some of the other girls unfortunate enough to work here, I'll pay you a visit when I come back."

Clint leaned forward slightly while staring into Holling's eyes as if he were glaring straight down into the man's soul. "In fact, if some nasty accident was to happen to me, your competition or your employees, I'll figure you're behind it and come for you."

"So what the hell am I supposed to do?" Holling squealed.

"Keep your nose clean and watch out for the girls who work for you. It may sound like a lot, but there's plenty of other men who do a real good job of it every day."

Clint smirked once more, which gave not one bit of comfort to Holling. As he stood up from his chair, Clint turned and looked to find all of the gunmen standing at various spots waiting for the signal from their boss. It didn't take much to see that they were all positioned with the knowledge that Clint would have to walk past every one of them if he intended on getting through the front door.

Tipping his hat to them, Clint walked between the card

tables and toward one of the closer gunmen. Clint's face was cold as a wall of ice, which was more than enough to freeze the gunman in his boots until some more of his friends were able to help.

Clint had no intention of waiting around that long and he had no intention of walking through the front door. At least, he wasn't going to use the front door that everyone else used.

Most people might have forgotten about the other door leading into the Cherry Blossom, just as they'd probably forgotten the place had actually once been two storefronts, with nothing more than a wall or two separating them. The construction was shoddy and chunks of those walls still remained. The other door might have been nailed shut, but that job was poorly done as well.

Clint pushed the door open hard enough to dislodge the nails. Plumes of brown dust spewed from the hinges amid a series of ear-splitting creaks. It was the only resistance Clint got as he left the Cherry Blossom.

TWELVE

The next morning, Clint woke up to the sound of some-one's knuckles pounding against his door. His hand reflex-ively went for the Colt stashed under his pillow and he was aiming the gun before his eyes had fully focused.

As if sensing the gun pointed at the door, the person knocking on the other side of it stopped and spoke in a gruff voice. "I know you're in there, Clint."

Recognizing Sal's voice, Clint lowered the gun and walked over to the door. He opened it carefully until he could get a look outside. Sal was alone, but he stormed in-side as if he had an entire posse behind him.

"Just what the hell have you been up to?" Sal growled as he stomped through the doorway.

"Good morning, Sal," Clint said.

Sal looked at the gun in Clint's hand, but didn't seem concerned by it in the least. "Last time I checked, the worst thing you woke up with was Jasmine."

"Sounds like you're jealous."

For one of the few times since Clint had met the big man, Sal grinned. "Yeah. Me and every other cowboy who struts in here thinking she's on the menu like the other girls."

"Jasmine runs your business pretty well. I wouldn't take the chance of upsetting her if she heard you talking like that."

Sal waved those words off as if he were swatting a horse's rump. "Eh, you're the fool if you think she doesn't know the torture she puts my customers through when she struts through here and refuses all the offers she gets."

"Is that why you almost knocked my door off its hinges?"

"No," Sal said as he tried to work himself back up into the lather he'd had a few moments ago. "I wanted to ask you what in the hell you thought you were doing by riling up Holling the way you did."

Pulling on his shirt, Clint began gathering up his things as he asked, "Did I upset him?"

"Don't bullshit me. You know goddamn well what you did. We had a nice little truce going. Since we don't exactly have the sympathetic ear of the law around here, that's about all that separates me and him from a shooting war."

"There's not going to be a war. Just settle down."

"And where the hell do you think you're going?" Sal asked as if he'd only just noticed what Clint was doing. "Looks like you're clearing out."

"I am."

"So you just shake up the hornet's nest and ride away? That's perfect."

"Do you even know about the girl who came here the other day crying about her missing sister?"

Sal's face lost some of its anger and he nodded. "Yeah. I heard."

"I'm going to track down that missing girl. Something tells me there'll be others."

"What makes you so sure?"

"What can you tell me about Coltraine and his Indian friends?"

"I can tell you that you don't want to be messing with

them. They're cold-blooded killers, Clint, and there's lots of 'em. You'd do well to stay here and fix the mess you've already got."

"There's no mess," Clint said. "Holling won't make a move because he's a coward and because it would be bad for business. He'll sit on his fat ass until he's got no other choice and you must know that just as well as I do."

Sal shrugged. "Holling may be easy to handle, but Coltraine and the men he rides with sure as hell ain't."

"What do you know of them?" Clint asked.

"Not a lot. I don't have a damn thing to do with their kind."

"I've heard that's a dangerous position to take."

Sal chuckled once and said, "That's why I got to try and get help from the likes of you whenever I can."

"Do you know where they go? Where they meet up? Where they come from? Anything at all?"

Taking another step into the small room, Sal dropped a hand on Clint's shoulder that felt more like a thick cut of beef. "I told you I don't have anything to do with them and that's the way it is. Now, you've done more than enough to make up for the money I loaned you. In fact, you did a hell of a lot more and I thank you for it."

"You run a nice place," Clint said. "The free beer was worth it."

"Then take some free advice, as well. Stay away from Coltraine. Some say he's got a whole tribe of redskins backing him up and I've heard nothing to dispute it. I may not be a fancy gunfighter, but I know you're the sort of man who dives into a fight and tries to figure his way out later. Someday you may just dive into something that you can't figure your way out of."

THIRTEEN

Even though Sal didn't have much to say regarding Coltraine, he was still more helpful than Holling. As Clint prepared to leave, Sal recounted the times Coltraine had come to pay him a visit. His story was similar to Holling's in most regards, except for the part where a girl was handed over as a quick way to get Coltraine to leave him alone. While Holling had looked on that as a cost of doing business, Sal considered it a filthy shame.

When Clint was ready to leave, Sal made sure he was well supplied with everything from food to blankets. In addition to all of that, he stopped Clint from leaving by taking hold of Eclipse's reins outside of Tad's.

"Here," Sal said as he thrust a thick fist up toward Clint. "Take this."

The moment Clint saw the money poking out from between Sal's fingers, he shook his head. "No need for that. We're square."

"Go on. You can work it off when you come back."

Tugging on Eclipse's reins, he got the black Darley Arabian moving away from Sal. "There's a bank along the way that's got enough to keep me going for a while, but thanks for the offer."

"Then why the hell didn't you go there to pay off yer goddamn debt?" Sal shouted as Clint rode away.

"Because," Clint replied as he twisted in his saddle to look over his shoulder, "I probably would have just spent my time in your place anyhow. Give my best to Jasmine."

Sal shook his head and waved dismissively. Even though Clint couldn't hear him, he knew well enough that the big man would be muttering to himself for a while.

Clint's intention had been to rest up and head out after a hearty breakfast and a talk with Sal, but since his schedule had been upended a bit, he rode out of Markton earlier than planned. One of the things that Sal's and Holling's stories had in common was the fact that Coltraine and the others he brought along with him usually arrived from the north and headed back that way when they left. While Clint fully intended on following that lead, he turned west as soon as he put Markton behind him.

He rode for a mile or two before finally spotting what he'd been looking for. The old farmhouse was so small that it practically blended in with every other shape on the horizon. Clint watched carefully as he approached, but saw no sign of life anywhere near the house. Even so, he brought Eclipse to a stop in front of the house and watched it from the saddle.

"It's Clint," he announced in a voice that shouldn't have carried too far. "Anyone hear me?"

One of the shutters was nudged open by the barrel of a rifle. A woman's face peered out from within the house and didn't relax until she got a good look at Clint for herself. Only then did Jill lower the rifle. "Stay right there and I'll let you in," she said.

"Don't bother," Clint replied. "I only came along to make sure you two got here all right."

Jill nodded. "We did. Kaylee's in here, cleaning up a bit. This was her pappy's house, so she knows where there's still some things we can use around here."

"Do you have enough food for a few days?"

"Maybe even a week. How long will we need to stay here?"

"Does anyone know you're the one taking Kaylee under your wing?"

"Actually, yes."

"Is Holling one of them?" Clint asked.

"No! The only ones who know about her wouldn't want to hurt her. The rest don't even care."

"Just so long as you know you can trust them."

Shaking her head, Jill told him, "Every last one of the girls consoled her just like every last one of them is helping us now. And it's not just the girls at the billiard hall. Alicia's friends from the Blossom are helping, too. They're even taking up a collection to get Kaylee out of here if there's too much trouble."

"That's not a bad idea. She might want to take them up on that offer."

"Why?" Jill asked as her face darkened. "Is there going to be more trouble?"

Clint saw Kaylee peeking out from another window. He gave her a wink and said, "I'll just have to see what I can do."

FOURTEEN

Clint rode west and headed for a wide pass he knew would cut all the way through the mountains. The place he was headed for was a good-sized town named Silver City. It was one of the many mining towns to benefit from a lucky strike, and one of the few to prosper after the miners had taken all they could find.

Off the top of his head, Clint could think of at least half a dozen more Silver Cities across the country, which made this one an ideal place for him to plant his own bit of silver. Rather than go to a stream or cave to dig it up, however, Clint rode into town and went to the Silver City Savings and Loan.

It was late afternoon when he arrived and the place was fairly quiet. When he walked into the little bank, Clint noticed more than a few tellers eyeing the gun at his side. Before they could get the wrong idea of why he was there, Clint said, "I'd like to make a withdrawal from my account."

Judging by the uncomfortable shifting of the skinny man behind the thin iron bars, those words weren't exactly calming. He relaxed once Clint went through the motions of withdrawing his money from a legitimate account. When he tipped his hat to conclude his business, Clint had money in his pocket and the bank hadn't been robbed, so everyone was happy.

Clint's next stop was a place a little ways down the street from the saloon where he normally drank when in town. The place was called the Peacock's Feather and was made up to be an elegant social club. None of the locals were fooled by the airs of propriety, however, since the women who conducted business there were usually wearing nothing more than a lacy slip and boots laced up to their knees.

Walking into the place, Clint was immediately enveloped in perfumed air from the three girls who happened to be available at the moment.

"You're the best thing we've seen in a long time," purred a busty brunette. "How about we curl up and get to know each other?"

"First, I'd like to see whoever owns this place," Clint said.

The brunette didn't even flinch as she continued to rub her hands along Clint's chest.

One of the other girls had dark hair as well, but a more slender figure. "You just got here and you've already got a complaint?" she asked.

Clint laughed and spread his arms so he could drape them over both of the ladies who'd spoken to him. "Right about now, I doubt I could think of a complaint if my life depended on it. I just need to speak to someone who might know about a man who might've come around trying to cut out a piece of this place for himself."

The brunette with the ample curves took hold of Clint's hand and guided it between her legs. "If you're looking for a piece," she whispered, "I've got one for you right here."

"Believe me," Clint said as he positioned himself so the brunette could only get ahold of his leg, "the man I'm asking about is someone you'll want me to catch."

"You're a bounty hunter?"

"Ooo," the slender one said. "I like bounty hunters."

"I'm after a man named Coltraine," Clint said before any more women could descend on him. "Any of you ladies heard of him?"

Clint could tell he'd struck a chord with every single woman close enough to hear him. Two of the three that were nearest to him lowered their eyes and started easing back. The one who stayed put was the busty brunette, but she suddenly wasn't so talkative.

Of course, one reason for the silence in the room might have been the appearance of a wiry old man who looked more like a tattered scarecrow than anything that should be up and moving on its own.

"You wanna pull his tallywacker before he pays, then I'll still expect my percentage," the old man squawked as he gripped onto the doorway connecting the front room to a study. "Even if it comes out of your own pockets, I'll still get my percentage!"

"I know, Silas," the brunette said. "How could I forget?"

Squinting at her like a bird contemplating when to pluck an eye from its socket, Silas quickly shifted his gaze to Clint. Some of his white hair was plastered down, while other pieces of it stuck out at odd angles from his speckled scalp. "This here's a place of business. You pick out someone you like and have yer fun. No free samples!"

"I'm not trying to get anything for free," Clint said as he sensed more and more anger inside that bony old man. "I'm just—"

"He was just about to come up to my room, Silas," the brunette interrupted. "That is, unless you intend on scaring him off."

Silas stared at them both for another few seconds and finally let out a disgruntled sigh. Shuffling around, he went back to whatever he'd been doing in the next room.

"Come on," the brunette said as she took Clint by the hand. "Let's get some privacy."

The Peacock's Feather was set up like a lavishly furnished home, complete with pictures on the walls and doilies on the tables. Like most houses of its kind, this one didn't hold up too well under close scrutiny. The pictures were all of various women in various stages of undress and it was plain to see that the only rooms used for more than show were the ones upstairs.

On the way up to one of those rooms, Clint asked, "Is that the man I need to talk to?"

"That's the man you were asking for," she corrected, "but I'm the one you need to talk to. You can call me Maddie."

"Do you know something about Co—"

For the second time since he'd arrived, Clint was cut off by Maddie. This time, she reached up to place her hand on his mouth while she glanced back in the direction from which they'd come. Suddenly, she took her hand away and planted a kiss on Clint's lips that truly curled his toes inside his boots.

Clint was so surprised that his eyes actually opened wider the longer she kissed him. That was how he was able to see Silas peeking out from the next room at them.

When Maddie started whispering to him, Clint could feel every movement of her lips against his own. "Silas won't like anyone asking about Coltraine, so unless you want to shoot that old man before he shoots you, come with me and look like you're happy about it."

Clint put on a smile and wrapped his arm around Maddie so she could lead him to her room. When he looked back again, Silas was still watching.

FIFTEEN

"Good Lord, these rooms are all starting to look the same," Clint groaned.

Maddie locked the door and set the key on top of a small table. "Visit a lot of cathouses, do ya?"

"Normally, I'd say no. Lately, I can't seem to get away from them."

Stepping in front of Clint, Maddie unbuttoned his shirt and slipped her fingers along his bare skin. "You don't look like the sort who would have to pay to catch a woman's eye."

Clint placed his hands on top of hers to keep her from undressing him any further. "If you've got something to say about Coltraine, just say it."

She put on an exaggerated frown and threw in a pouting lip to boot. "You sure you don't want to give this bed something to creak about?"

"That's beside the point. I came to talk about Coltraine and if you don't start talking, I'll march out of here and tell your boss how you duped me into coming up here."

She shrugged and kept trying to ease her fingers deeper underneath Clint's shirt.

"Then," he added, "I'll be sure to tell him that I got away without paying."

Finally, Maddie pulled her hands away and moved to the only chair in the room. After placing the chair quietly next to the little square window, she said, "You wouldn't do that. I can spot an asshole a mile away and you're not one."

Clint took a breath and let it out in frustration. "Great. This has been a waste of time."

"Coltraine was here two weeks ago," Maddie announced.

"Was he alone?"

"He's never alone. He brought an Indian along as always, but not one of the Indians from around here."

"You know that for certain?" Clint asked.

Maddie laughed once and nodded. "This town's a stone's throw from two Shoshone villages. It helps to know your neighbors."

"What was Coltraine here for?"

"Same thing as always. He wanted Silas to hand over one of the girls and that old piece of shit was more than willing to comply."

"Does he always hand over a woman when Coltraine comes around asking for one?"

"Nope. Sometimes he hands over two. It never really bothers him, though, because they're usually fresh off a train or lost on their way to Cheyenne."

"We're a long ways from Cheyenne," Clint pointed out.

Maddie nodded. "They're really lost."

"How often does he come around?"

"Maybe once every couple of months. No more than twice in that amount of time, though."

"And you're sure about this?" Clint asked.

"I've been working here for three years. Silas may be a crusty old buzzard, but he's not dumb enough to get rid of one of his top earners. Besides, I've been helping him balance the books ever since his eyes started to go. That's why he doesn't trust me."

After his brief time in the old man's company, Clint had an easier time swallowing that odd bit of logic. Before he could ask another question, Clint saw her hold up a finger and point toward the door. Suddenly, Maddie let out a loud moan that sounded as if she were having the time of her life.

"He'll come knocking if he doesn't think we're conducting business in here," Maddie said softly.

"I'm looking for Coltraine and one of the women he took from Markton."

"If you find him, you might have more than one woman who's ready to leave."

"How many do you think there might be?"

"I don't know his schedule or how many places he hits on each trip," Maddie admitted. "But I do know he hits a lot of places in all. If someone is doing something about it, I'm willing to help. Unfortunately, Silas likes his arrangement with Coltraine, which is why I brought you up here to talk. Odds are Silas would find some way to get word to Coltraine if he knew you were after him. I figure, you being the Gunsmith and all, that you're the best bet we've got."

"You know me?"

"Sure," Maddie replied. "One of the new girls used to work at the Cherry Blossom and she told us all about how Sal hired you on to protect his girls. I always did like Sal. Anyway, all I can tell you is that Coltraine always passes through Fort Marsden just south of the Montana border."

"Fort Marsden?"

"It's more of a trading post, but a few soldiers have set up shop of their own. They take money to escort folks through Indian country, but I'm sure they're up to plenty more than that."

"And how did you come by this information?"

"Let's just say I've spent a few springtimes earning some extra money by providing some of those boys company. Silas had that one worked out way before I started working here. I happened to be working when Coltraine was carting some of his stolen girls north to the Crow."

"So the Crow Indians are working with him?"

"I wouldn't think all of them are, but there's sure a few. I know the ones Coltraine rides with are Crow."

Clint's head swam with all the new information he was being given. The feeling reminded him of the old warning to beware what you wish for, because you might just get it. "How many others are there besides Coltraine?"

"I couldn't tell you," Maddie said regretfully. "I know that he travels with one Indian when he makes his rounds, but it's rarely the same one twice in a row."

"Is there anyone who might know the answer?"

"There's a supply sergeant named Bray who would know plenty about Coltraine's comings and goings. He's stationed at Fort Marsden and you should have some time to get there since Coltraine is off collecting a few more girls before heading back north."

"Are you sure?"

She nodded. "I make it my business to know, just in case someone finally decides to do something about it."

Suddenly, someone rapped on the door as if they were trying to crack the boards.

"Open this door," Silas squawked from the hall.

"Jesus Christ," Clint whispered. "Does he keep such a close eye on everyone you bring up here?"

"He gets jumpy around the time when Coltraine is around," she explained.

"How jumpy?"

"Jumpy enough to keep a pistol on him when he goes to the outhouse and jumpy enough to kill someone who he thinks might spoil his deal with Coltraine or send him to jail for it."

The knocking came again, followed by Silas's grating voice. "That's the gunfighter from Sal's place. I know it is! Open up!" After a half second of silence, there came the metallic scraping of a key moving in the door's lock.

SIXTEEN

After fumbling with the key, Silas pushed open the door with one hand. His other hand was wrapped around an old Smith & Wesson revolver that looked as if it weighed more than he did. His eyes were flaring and he bared his teeth like a mongoose looking for something to bite.

"If you're up here spreading lies about . . ." Silas stopped himself in midsentence when he finally stepped into the room. The old man's eyes snapped open a bit when he got a look at Clint and Maddie.

Clint was sitting on the edge of the bed and Maddie was on her knees between his legs. Her head was in his lap and both of her hands were sliding up and down Clint's thighs. Slowly, Maddie raised her head and looked over her shoulder.

"What in the hell do you think you're doing?" Clint snarled.

Looking around as if the room were big enough to host another group of conspirators, Silas mumbled, "Oh, I thought that there was . . . that you two would be . . ."

"What did you think I came here for?" Clint asked. "To have a gun pointed at me by some crazy old fool?"

Silas lowered the pistol as if he'd forgotten it was in his hand. Squinting at Clint, he said, "Sorry about that. I must have thought you were someone else."

So far, Maddie was enjoying watching the show. Turning just enough for Silas to catch a glimpse of her stroking Clint's erection, she asked, "Should I leave you two alone or can we get back to what we were doing?"

Some of the fire returned to Silas's eyes, but that wasn't nearly enough to overpower the glare he was getting from Clint. "My apologies," Silas said, while backing away and bumping against the door frame in the process. "I'll go."

Not only did Silas pull the door shut, but he took the time to fumble with the key some more so he could lock it, as well. After that, the sound of his footsteps rattled through the air as he rushed back down the stairs.

"I don't think I've ever seen him so flustered," Maddie said. "That was one hell of a sight."

"Quick thinking on your part. I wasn't looking forward to gunning down a frail old man today." Clint started to get up, but Maddie wasn't about to move. "Do you think he'll be coming back?"

She smiled and shook her head, then slowly brushed her lips back and forth against the tip of his penis. "He'll be watching for us to come down the stairs, but he won't be barging in on us."

"Then you don't have to—"

"No," she said as she slid him into her mouth and out again, "but I want to."

Clint tried to maintain his focus on the task at hand since Maddie had already proven to be so helpful. "So . . . Coltraine is probably getting women and trading them to another tribe."

Maddie nodded just enough for her mouth to rub against

him at a slightly different angle. She kept one hand moving up and down over Clint's stomach while the other rested in his lap. When she slid her lips down his cock again, she ran her tongue along the bottom of it.

As the pleasure rushed through him, Clint leaned back on his elbows and pulled in a deep breath. The more she sucked on him, the harder it was for him to remember any other reason for him to be there. Finally, he asked, "Is there anything else . . . you can tell me?"

Although Maddie let him slip from her mouth, she kept her lips less than inch from his stiff cock and her hands moving up and down along its length. "I've told you all I know. If there's anything else, I'm sure it'll come to me if I take a few moments to think."

Her lips immediately closed around the tip of his cock while her hand vigorously stroked him. The moment she took her hand away, she lowered her head all the way down until every last inch of him slid down her throat. Maddie curled the tip of her tongue as she eased her head back up again, sending a chill through Clint's entire body in the process.

"I figure this is the least I can do for a man who's out to put down a mangy dog like Coltraine," Maddie whispered. "If there's anything else I can do, you just tell me."

Clint sat up so he could run his fingers through Maddie's hair. "I want to get moving as soon as I can before those girls are lost for good."

"Fort Marsden is only a hard day's ride from here. You should be able to make it before Coltraine manages to get there."

"And I guess it wouldn't look right if we came down the stairs right away," Clint said. "With Silas watching and all."

"That's right." With that, Maddie placed her lips around Clint's hard cock and slid them all the way down. Her head bobbed up and down faster and faster. She only slowed when she felt Clint's hand press against the back of her head. From there, she eased up so she could give him something he wouldn't soon forget.

SEVENTEEN

When Maddie had told him Fort Marsden was a hard day's ride away, Clint figured he'd leave Silver City as soon as possible. Once his legs were steady enough to walk again, he left Maddie's room and headed downstairs for the front door. Sure enough, Silas was watching from the other room and muttered something under his breath when Clint tipped his hat and left.

Eclipse was waiting outside and responded eagerly when Clint climbed into the saddle and flicked the reins. The stallion tore through town and seemed anxious to break into a run. Once Clint found the trail headed north, he touched his heels to Eclipse's sides and gave the stallion exactly what he'd been waiting for.

In no time at all, Eclipse had built up a head of steam that made Clint feel more like he was flying than riding. The directions Maddie had given him were simple enough and every one of the landmarks she'd mentioned were right where they should be. Considering how accommodating she'd been and that she was among the women who were being threatened, Clint had no reason to think she was lying to him. Even so, he kept his eyes and ears open for any sign of an ambush.

Not only was there no ambush, but Clint caught first sight of the fort by early evening. When he saw it, he pulled back on the reins and brought Eclipse to a stop. Clint took a spyglass from his saddlebag, peered through the lenses and nodded to himself.

"Sure looks like a fort to me," Clint said under his breath. "Not a very impressive one, but a fort all the same."

He climbed down from his saddle and took a moment to stretch his legs. After taking a few sips from his canteen, he cupped his hand to pour some of the water into it. "I guess when she said it was a hard day's ride away," he said as he held the water under Eclipse's mouth, "she was talking about a stagecoach ride."

As the Darley Arabian lapped up the water and nudged him for more, Clint did some quick figuring in his head.

While giving the stallion another helping of water, Clint nodded again. "Yep. That would be about a day's ride by stage and there's no such thing as an easy day's ride by stage."

When Eclipse stopped drinking, Clint took another sip for himself and put the canteen away. He considered camping outside for the night, just so he could be rested in the morning. Then again, if the fort was as Maddie described it, there may just be a much better alternative.

When Clint approached the fort, he watched for the usual patrols and guards. There were no patrols and the post where a guard normally sat was occupied by a tired-looking man in a dirty uniform. Clint instinctively slowed when passing the post, but the man there didn't even seem to notice him. Instead of vying for the guard's attention, Clint moseyed through the open gates.

Inside, the place had the vague structure of many other forts Clint had seen. There were small buildings around the perimeter and close to the wall, with larger structures in the middle. Unlike those other forts, however, this one had little to no military presence.

Apart from the sleepy guard, Clint counted less than half a dozen other men in uniform. There were several other folks wandering around, but they were either civilians or very casual army personnel. Further strengthening what Maddie had told him, there were signs nailed to the larger structures over the markings that had been there before.

The blockhouse was now a dry good's store and the officer's quarters had apparently been converted into a hotel or boardinghouse. The stables were still intact, but now charged for their services. There were a few buildings that weren't labeled, but Clint didn't need a sign to tell what a saloon looked like. He also had to assume there was some place where the working girls could be found, since he didn't see many women moving about in the open.

As much as Clint wanted to find Sergeant Bray, he decided not to ride in and draw attention right away. Instead, he put Eclipse up in the livery and asked the man taking the fees where he could find something to do.

"Just follow yer ears," the liveryman told him. "You want liquor, listen for the drunks. You want a woman, listen for them, too. It ain't like you can get lost around here."

Oddly enough, that lazy explanation came from one of the few men actually wearing a uniform.

When Clint stepped outside again, he caught sight of a short man leaning against the building directly across from the livery. Clint took two steps in that direction, which was enough to cause the man to turn and walk away.

Although Clint hadn't gotten too long of a look, he could tell the man was an Indian. After circling around that building, Clint couldn't find a trace of him.

EIGHTEEN

Although the liveryman wasn't very detailed in his directions, they turned out to be all Clint needed. The signs nailed over the originals were either too cracked to read or written in paint so old and cheap that it had flaked off to the point of being illegible. But all Clint needed to do was follow his ears.

The saloon sounded like most other saloons at this time of night. There were loud voices and the sounds of someone trying to play a banjo coming from inside a narrow building in the center of the fort. But Clint was drawn more to the large square building, which had to have been the enlisted men's quarters.

That building was two floors tall and had several of the upper, front windows knocked completely out. Inside those windows, he could see women sitting and fanning themselves while tossing lazy smiles down at him. There was plenty to listen to as well, since some of the more enthusiastic women were doing their best to make their current customers feel good about whatever they were doing.

Clint glanced up at the women in the windows, but didn't return their smiles. Instead, he looked at them the way a rancher would inspect his herd. He kept that businesslike expression on his face as he walked inside and stepped up to the first person who looked as if they worked there.

The inside of the place was unlike any of the other cathouses Clint had been to recently. While most others looked like actual houses, this one looked as if it had been put through very few changes since it was under official army jurisdiction. Apart from a few decorations thrown here and there, the place still felt like a barracks. The halls were narrow. The doors were many and evenly spaced. There was still even the smell of boot polish in the air.

"Hello there," a middle-aged, brown-haired woman said as she stepped in from the next room. "Did you just arrive?"

"Yes. I'm here to meet up with a friend of mine."

The woman wore a plain dress that was buttoned low enough to show a generous amount of cleavage, but not low enough to show much else. "We've got plenty of friendly girls here."

"It's not a girl I'm after."

The woman raised her eyebrows and cocked her head slightly.

"And it's not like that, either," Clint clarified. "I'm here on business. The man I'm to meet should either be here already or might have passed through recently. His name's Coltraine."

When she heard that, the woman's face lost all of its friendliness. "Oh. He hasn't been around yet."

"Is he expected?"

"Yes," she replied, as if she were referring to an infection that was being passed around. "But he's not here yet. If you want to wait for him, you'll have to do it somewhere else."

Clint could hear the disgust dripping from the woman's tone. He felt a fair amount of it himself, simply due to the part he was playing. As much as he wanted to tell her what he was really after, Clint was too close to slip up now. If he'd learned anything during his visits to these cathouses, it was that it was safest to assume someone was keeping an eye on what was going on.

"I'll check back later," Clint said. "If he does come around, I'd like to be told about it."

At first, the woman looked as if she fully intended on telling Clint to stuff his request up his ass. Then, a twinge of fear showed in the corner of her eye as she nodded and lowered her eyes. "Will you be staying at the hotel or at the saloon?"

"The saloon."

"Fine."

Clint knew he was playing a role and knew he wouldn't let that role harm anyone in any way. He also knew that it felt like shit to be looked at as just another one of the scum in Coltraine's line of work.

"Here," he said while holding out a few dollars to the woman. "Take this for your trouble."

The woman looked surprised when she saw the money and grateful once she had it in her own hands. The fear quickly returned, however, after she tucked the money away. "I'll be sure to let you know when he arrives."

"Thanks."

Clint left the cathouse and stepped outside. The air was cooling off a bit, but not enough to make him feel comfortable. He took the next few minutes to walk around the fort and familiarize himself with the layout. Just as the liveryman had promised, there wasn't much to see.

Despite what he'd told the woman in the cathouse, Clint had no intention of staying in a room at the saloon. If anything, he would rent a room in whatever passed for a hotel there. That way, he could watch the saloon without having to sleep there in case the wrong person heard about his arrangement and decided to kill him in his sleep.

Actually, the more he thought about it, the more Clint

figured he wouldn't sleep anywhere inside the fort's walls. The whole place had a dirty feel to it as though the air itself were filthy.

As he walked around, Clint found two small buildings that weren't being used for anything. One of those was a smaller stable that had probably been used for officer's horses or possibly overflow from the regular livery. At the moment, it was dark, empty, and wasn't far from the saloon. That meant it was a perfect place for Clint to stand and wait for Coltraine to arrive.

Maddie had given him a description of Coltraine before he'd left, but Clint just had to keep his fingers crossed that it would be enough to pick the man out when he arrived. At the very least, he guessed he should at least be able to spot the Indian he traveled with or the women that were his prisoners.

Clint barely had a chance to get comfortable leaning against the darkened doorway when he heard soft footsteps creeping up behind him. As soon as he began to turn and have a look, Clint was stopped by the metallic click of a pistol's hammer being cocked back.

"Don't move another muscle, asshole," a voice behind him hissed, "or you'll get your first shot in the balls before I burn you down."

NINETEEN

"That's no way for a lady to talk," Clint said as he raised his hands and turned around.

The voice that he'd heard was a cross between a whisper and a snarl. It cut through the air like an arrow. The face that went along with it was a whole lot prettier, even if it was twisted into a serious frown.

"What made you think I was a lady?" she asked.

"Because women will be the first ones to threaten to shoot a man in that particular spot."

"Like you're all such a bunch of gentlemen?"

"Not hardly. We just don't like to think about something like that."

Clint kept his hands up, but was prepared to pluck his modified Colt from its holster at any moment. Although the woman's gun was still pointed at him, he didn't think he would have to return the favor. In fact, he kept his hands high and unmoving just to stay on her good side.

The woman stepped forward slowly and stopped well outside of arm's reach. The gun in her hand was a newer model, small enough for her to manage and still plenty big enough to be a threat. What struck Clint even more was the fact that she handled that gun as if she'd had plenty of practice.

"What are you doing hiding in the shadows?" Clint asked.

"I was just going to ask you the same thing."

"Is there a law against a man wanting some peace and quiet to go along with his fresh air?"

"No, but there is a law against kidnapping innocent women."

Clint squinted into the darkness to get a better look at her. His eyes had become adjusted to the night, but the woman was still shrouded in shadows so thick that they almost completely eclipsed her. "If I wanted to make a move for my gun, I could do it whether you're here or one step closer."

"And either way, you'd be just as dead."

"Exactly."

Reluctantly, the woman stepped forward just enough for some of the pale light from outside to fall over her. She had a trim body and appeared to be in her late twenties. Her blond hair was slightly tousled, but still framed her face nicely. Although her eyes were narrowed suspiciously, it would have been impossible to hide their beauty.

"Are you going to shoot me or should we start this off on a more friendly note?" Clint asked.

"I haven't decided yet. What were you doing a few minutes ago?"

"You mean at the cathouse?"

"That's right," she said with a curt nod.

"Something tells me you already know the answer to that."

The blonde was quiet as she studied Clint even more. Her eyes moved up and down over him, lingering slightly over the gun at his side. "Take out that gun and toss it to me."

Clint's hand slowly lowered and stopped when he saw her arm tense and her grip tighten around her pistol.

"Two fingers only," she warned.

Using his thumb and forefinger, Clint lifted the Colt from its holster and tossed it forward. The gun landed with a thump in the straw at her feet. Rather than bend down to pick it up, she placed her foot on top of it and kept her aim fixed upon Clint's chest.

"Who are you?" she asked.

"My name's Clint Adams. What about you?"

"Rachel Dovetree. Does that sound familiar?"

Clint shook his head, which only caused the blonde to scowl and straighten her gun arm as if she were getting ready to fire.

"I guess men like you wouldn't even care to know the names of the women you steal. Probably makes it easier to cart them around and sell them off like so much god-damned property."

"What do you know about that?"

"I know plenty," Rachel snapped. "Just like I know that you've been trying to meet up with that son of a bitch Coltraine since the moment you got here."

"I've been looking for Coltraine. Tracking him down, not joining up with him if that's what you think."

"I think Coltraine deserves to die, but I'll settle for one of his friends to hold me over until I can get to him."

Clint caught sight of someone running to the saloon and quickly recognized the woman from the cathouse he'd paid to alert him about Coltraine's whereabouts. Rachel's eyes glanced away as well, but she was looking at something else outside of the stable.

"Looks like some of your other friends are here, too, Clint Adams," she said smugly. "I might be able to drop more of you tonight than I bargained on."

Suddenly, Clint realized tossing his gun away was less of an act of good faith and more of a stupid, possibly fatal, mistake.

TWENTY

"Don't say a damn thing to your friends out there," Rachel said, "and I might just let you walk out of this."

"They're not my friends," Clint insisted. "I came to track them down just like you."

"Bullshit. Just keep your mouth shut."

"Take me hostage," Clint offered.

"What?"

"We've got to do something before they get away. I don't know how long they'll stay here. Do you?"

Rachel was quiet as she nervously glanced back and forth between Clint and the outside. When he looked in the same direction that she did, Clint could finally see a pair of men walking from the cathouse to one of the smaller buildings that were away from the busier half of the fort.

"Whatever they're doing here, I doubt they'll stay long," Clint said. "You can either let me have my gun and we can do this together, or you can take me hostage if you think I'm one of them. Either way, you need to decide right now!"

"Dammit," Rachel said under her breath.

Clint looked back to where she was staring and saw the

two men had stopped short of one of the buildings. They were now talking to another pair of men and pointing toward the cathouse. The first pair continued into the smaller building while the second pair began walking briskly toward the cathouse.

When Clint turned around again, Rachel was directly beside him. The next thing he felt was the barrel of her pistol jabbing him in the ribs.

"You say or do one thing I don't like and I pull this trigger," she said. "Now tell me who the hell you really are."

"I told you already."

"I've followed you since Silver City and I know damn well you've been making the same stops as Coltraine."

"I'm tracking him."

"Then how do you know exactly where to go?"

"I've had a lot of practice," Clint explained. "Besides, Coltraine takes his victims from places like Silver City and the other women who work there are fed up with seeing it happen. They've been the ones that have helped me the most. Surely you must know something about that."

"Are you calling me a whore?"

"Jesus Christ," Clint growled. "If you're looking for an excuse to shoot, just do it already. You obviously have a stake in this or you wouldn't be here right now. I want to work with you, so either let me help or let me do what I came to do."

"Why should I trust you?"

"Because, unless you're very good with that gun, you're going to need my help when those two Indians get here."

Rachel looked away from Clint and saw that the second pair of men had already left the cathouse and were approaching the saloon. The woman who'd been there to try and find Clint was on her way out and the two men stepped right up to her so they could grab her by the arms. The men were Indians, all right. Their long, straight, black hair hung down past their shoulders and the pale moonlight was just bright enough for their dark complexions to be seen.

As Clint watched the Indians shove the woman around, he felt his hands ball into fists and the muscles in his jaw tighten. He couldn't hear what they were saying to her, but he had a feeling it wasn't good. Those feelings were confirmed when the woman finally broke down and started pointing to the saloon and explaining something in a quick rush of words.

"She was supposed to get me at the saloon when Coltraine arrived," Clint explained. "My guess is that's exactly what she's telling them right now."

"So you were here to meet Coltraine," Rachel stated.

"If I was, I'd be in that saloon where I told that woman I'd be instead of out here watching it the same way you were watching me."

Rachel thought that over as her eyes shifted from Clint to the two Indians outside the saloon. The longer she watched, the rougher those Indians got with the woman. By now, that woman's cries were getting loud enough to be heard in the abandoned stables.

"Those two are getting impatient out there," Clint said. "If you don't want to work with me, that's fine. But I'm not going to stand by here while that poor woman is pushed around on my account. If you want to stop me, you'll just have to shoot me in the back."

Without waiting for a response, Clint turned his back on Rachel and stepped out of the livery. He stopped and waved his arms over his head. "Hey there!" he shouted. "You two! I think I'm the one you're after!"

The Indians looked at him quickly and then looked back to the woman. She glanced at Clint and then started nodding and pointing to the saloon and the cathouse as if retracing her and Clint's steps. The Indians seemed to believe her because they pushed her aside hard enough to knock her down and walked toward the stables.

Clint's hand dropped reflexively to the holster at his side, only to find it empty. He kept his hand in place on top of the holster to cover it so at least the Indians couldn't tell he was unarmed.

As the Indians walked closer, the moonlight allowed Clint to see more details about their appearance. Both of them had large knives hanging from their belts. One had a pistol at his side while another had a rifle strapped to his back. They wore regular buttoned shirts that hung open to reveal muscled chests, but their pants were more traditional animal hide leggings.

As they got closer, both Indians placed their hands over a weapon in preparation for a fight.

"What is your business with us?" the taller of the two Indians asked.

"I've got some women to trade," Clint replied. "Let me talk to Coltraine."

Suddenly, Rachel exploded from the stable with her gun at the ready. "I knew it!" she shouted.

Clint reacted as quickly as he could to make sure the situation didn't go from bad to worse. Then again, it was hard to imagine how the situation could get any worse.

TWENTY-ONE

Clint's first impulse was to twist on the balls of his feet and grab the gun from Rachel's hand. She was so focused on the two Indians that she barely even saw Clint coming and didn't even notice her gun was gone until a full second later.

Shoving Rachel back into the stables, Clint looked over his shoulder and said, "Come in here and help me with this."

Rachel was kicking and swinging her fists even as she stumbled over a bale of hay. Clint rushed forward and began swearing at her as well as a bunch of others who weren't even there. All of this created a mix of confusion and curiosity that was just enough to get the Indians moving inside as well.

As both Indians stepped into the stables, their grip tightened around their weapons. That way, when Clint turned Rachel's pistol on them, they were able to react in a heartbeat. The bigger one pulled a machete out of its scabbard. The smaller one drew a .45, but wasn't able to clear leather before Clint slammed his knuckles against the man's wrist.

As the smaller Indian struggled to retract his battered arm, Clint wrapped one hand around his neck and shoved his back against a wall. The Indian's eyes were wide with surprise, but he wasn't surprised enough to keep from delivering a few blows of his own.

Clint barely managed to squirm to one side before the smaller Indian brought up his knee. Although the knee didn't land in its intended spot, it still grazed along Clint's hip and pounded against his lower ribs. Clint tried to bring his gun around to point it at the Indian's head before the Indian got to the knife he was reaching for.

But he didn't make it. The Indian removed his knife from its scabbard and swiped up toward Clint's chest in one fluid motion.

Meanwhile, the bigger Indian, who had been caught off guard when Clint lunged for his partner's gun, regained focus and reared back his machete to bury it in Clint's back. He stopped when he saw movement from the corner of his eye and was just quick enough to avoid getting attacked by Rachel.

Having drawn a knife of her own, she stabbed straight in toward the big Indian's midsection. Her teeth were bared and there was more than enough force behind her attack to make her a genuine threat. Even so, the big Indian had an amused smile on his face as he twisted out of the way.

"I don't know who you are," the big Indian said to her, "but you'll wish you hadn't done that."

Clint backed up a few steps and watched the knife in the smaller Indian's hand. He twitched again in response to a few quick feints, but saw the Indian back up the real slash with every muscle in his upper body. When the smaller Indian's blade swiped toward him again, Clint stepped aside and grabbed his attacker's wrist just above that incoming blade with the same speed he would have drawn his modified Colt.

Without losing his momentum, Clint turned the smaller Indian's knife back toward him and drove the blade into its owner's gut. Looking straight into the Indian's eyes, Clint shoved the blade in deeper until he felt the other man crumple. Before the body hit the floor, Clint turned to see the bigger Indian smacking the blade from Rachel's hand as if he were disciplining a child.

Clint dropped to one knee so he could take the knife from the hand of the dead Indian on the floor. Snapping his arm like a whip, Clint sent the blade spinning through the air to lodge into the bigger Indian's back. But rather than drop the Indian, Clint's efforts only seemed to make him madder.

The big Indian reached around to feel the knife lodged in the bone of his shoulder. His eyes took on an angry fire as he brought his huge machete up over his head. Clint could tell by the big Indian's stance that he didn't intend on turning away from Rachel. On the contrary, the Indian looked ready to finish her off and then tend to Clint.

Rather than let the big Indian do what he pleased, Clint got up and ran straight toward him. He tossed Rachel's gun to the floor, used his right hand to grab hold of the big Indian's arm while it was still raised and, with his left hand, grabbed hold of the knife still lodged in the Indian's shoulder.

It was obvious that the big Indian was strong enough to pull his arm free in a matter of seconds, so Clint twisted the knife in the the big Indian's back until he reacted to the pain. Giving the knife one more turn weakened the big Indian just enough for Clint to rip the machete from his hand.

As much as Clint wanted to drop the machete and pick up the gun he'd dropped, he wasn't keen on the idea of lowering himself so close to the big Indian's legs. Although the large man was heaving and unsteady thanks to the pain in his back, he was already pulling himself together.

"Here," Clint said as he kicked the gun toward Rachel. "Take this and keep him covered, but don't shoot unless you have to."

Rachel picked up the gun as soon as she could. Her first

instinct was to point it at the big Indian, but her aim soon began to shift between the Indian and Clint.

By this time, the big Indian had managed to get his fingers on the knife in his back and finally pull it out. As soon as the bloody knife was in his hand, he flipped it around so he was holding it by the blade as if he were ready to throw it.

Rachel pointed her gun at the Indian. "Don't even think about throwing that knife," she warned.

The Indian lowered his arm and relaxed a bit.

When Rachel looked for Clint, she was unable to find him. Her finger tensed on the trigger, but she knew better than to take her eyes off the Indian for more than a second. She found out the hard way that even a second was too long.

The big Indian's hand snapped up like it was springloaded and, just as he was about to send the knife into Rachel, he felt a dull thump on the back of his head.

Having watched where Rachel threw his Colt, Clint was able to find it and crack it against the Indian's skull before the knife was thrown. It took another crack from the pistol butt to drop the Indian to his knees. After that, Clint had one very angry woman to contend with.

TWENTY-TWO

"What the hell are you doing?" Rachel asked.

Clint had already dropped his Colt back in its holster and was rushing to the door of the livery to get a look outside. "What's it look like I'm doing?"

"Looks like you might be looking for your friends to arrive."

"What friends?"

"I don't know!" Rachel said as she shuffled away from Clint and both Indians, her back to a wall. "First, I thought you were one of them, then I think you might not be, then you take my gun, and now . . . I don't know what the hell to think!"

Clint held out his hand and waved it at her while crouching and studying the people moving throughout the fort. "Keep your voice down."

"You'd better start telling me what you're up to, or I'll make plenty of noise with this gun in my hand."

Satisfied that there was nobody else in the abandoned livery, Clint walked back inside. He faced Rachel with both hands held open at waist level. His voice was smooth and calm. "I had to take your gun before you fired a shot. We don't know how many more of these assholes are around, so we shouldn't draw any more attention to ourselves."

"You left me without a weapon," she said angrily. "I could have been killed."

"You had a knife. Besides," Clint added with a shrug, "I did give your gun back."

"What about calling them over here after you shoved me back? You were asking them to help you."

"I also said there were more women in here with me. What would you have preferred? That I tell them to please step a little closer so I could stab one of them and knock the other over his head until he drops? I doubt that would have gone over too well."

"Why did they come to you?" she asked suspiciously. "It seemed like they trusted you."

Clint let out an aggravated sigh as he looked down at the big man laying on the floor. So far, the Indian was remaining still, but Clint didn't expect that to last forever. "They didn't know me and there's no way in hell you haven't realized that already. If you're looking for an excuse to pull the trigger, you're not going to find a good one. What you're going to have to do is trust me for a little while."

"Why should I trust you?"

"Because," Clint said as his hand snapped down and came back up with the modified Colt in his grasp, "I could have killed you at any time if that's what I wanted to do."

Rachel's eyes darted to the gun in her hands, but quickly returned to Clint. He'd cleared leather so quickly that she had barely seen him move. The fact that she hadn't jumped and pulled her trigger was only because she skipped being surprised and went straight to being frozen in place.

She only let out her breath when she saw Clint smile and lower the Colt back into its holster. "How did you know these two would show?"

"I told a woman at the cathouse to come get me at the

saloon when Coltraine arrived. Then I came here to watch the saloon and see when the woman came back. That way, even if someone asked her where I was, they wouldn't know the truth any more than she did."

"And what were you intending to do when Coltraine did arrive?" Rachel asked. "Crack him on the back of his head with your gun?"

"Actually . . . I was kind of making this up as I go along. All I wanted to do was get some idea of what's really going on and where these missing girls are being taken."

"I know where they are being taken," Rachel said. "They are being traded off to the Crow like a bunch of cattle."

"Do you know *exactly* where they are being taken?" Clint asked. "Because that's the sort of thing we need to know if we're going to find those women."

Still staring along the sights of her pistol, Rachel slowly shook her head. "I don't know exactly."

Clint grinned and knelt down beside the big, unconscious Indian. "Well, this one right here does. And since we managed to knock him out without calling all his friends over here in the process, we can wake him up and ask him."

"Wake him up?"

"After some precautions, of course. See if you can find some rope."

TWENTY-THREE

When the big Indian opened his eyes, the first thing he saw was Clint's smiling face.

"Rise and shine," Clint said.

The Indian's first instinct was to jump to his feet and get his hands wrapped around Clint's throat. The moment he tried to do that, however, was the same moment he realized he'd been hog-tied with double the amount of knots required to keep a full-grown bull from going anywhere. Because of that, the Indian only succeeded in flopping on the floor like a fish that had been pulled out of a stream.

"You'd better settle down, big fella," Clint said, "or my friend there will be forced to put you down."

The Indian looked to where Clint was motioning and saw Rachel standing with a pistol in each hand. Her eyes were fierce and both guns were perfectly steady.

"In case you're wondering," Clint said, "you've been out long enough for your friends to give up on you. Actually, they might not have given up, but they're not in the fort anymore."

"What do you want?" the Indian asked. "You must want something or you wouldn't be here."

"Very observant. I'd like to know what Coltraine's been up to lately. I want to know how many women he's got, where they are now and where they're going."

"Why should I tell you?"

"I thought we've already covered that," Clint said, nodding back toward Rachel, who still sighted down both pistols.

The Indian squared his jaw and shifted so he was looking straight up at the roof. After that, he might as well have been a log with rope wrapped around it.

"You're not going to talk?" Clint asked.

The Indian stayed mute.

"Fine. Maybe you'd like to be reacquainted with another friend of yours."

Clint disappeared from the Indian's view for a moment. When he reappeared, he was holding the machete that had been brought into the livery by the Indian himself. Clint wielded the blade like he was cutting through dense bushes. His final slice was purposely aimed to pass within an inch of the Indian's nose.

"Maybe I should test my aim with this thing," Clint said. "To be honest, though, I don't think I'm very good."

"Bray won't let you do this," the Indian said. "Even if you kill me, he'll hunt you down, and Coltraine will put a price on your head."

"Are you talking about Sergeant Bray?"

The Indian looked up at Clint and then went silent once more.

Clint hunkered down to the Indian's level and announced, "You've really only got two choices here. You tell us what we need, or we bury you under this floor."

"You'll kill me anyway. I can see that much in the woman's eyes."

Clint looked over to Rachel and had to admit that he saw the same thing. "Fine," he said with a shrug. "If you insist on protecting Coltraine, I think that's real admirable.

Especially considering how long you've been gone and how he just rode off without so much as searching the fort for you. I mean, this isn't a very big place."

"If they'd left, you would already know where they've gone."

"I've followed Coltraine long enough. I want to know where he's headed and I want to know where he takes the women. You'll be saving me some time by telling me this and I'd cut you loose as a way to thank you. Otherwise, I know some officers at another army post who would be real happy to see you. Some of those cavalry men enjoy getting the occasional live Indian for a change. You're a big fella, so you might even stay alive for a good day or two once they start in on you."

After a pause, the Indian said, "Help me sit up."

Clint obliged and hauled the Indian so he could sit as normally as he could considering he was still tied up.

After settling into his new position, the Indian looked directly into Clint's eyes and said, "Before you go after Shadow Walker, you must decide if you're prepared to die."

"Shadow Walker?"

The Indian nodded.

"You mean Coltraine?" Clint asked.

"Among the Crow, he is known as Shadow Walker. Someone gave him that name because he drifts from place to place without leaving a trace. When he falls over something, or someone, that thing disappears."

"Or that person?"

Again, the Indian nodded. "Even among my people, he is feared. He's collected followers from many tribes and he's proven himself in blood."

Rachel let out a humorless laugh. "I suppose you're going to tell me he's some kind of warrior?"

"No," the Indian replied as he shifted his eyes toward her. He ignored the guns in her hands and looked straight into her eyes without a hint of fear.

For a moment, Rachel even forgot about the guns she held. In that bit of time, it seemed entirely possible that the Indian would jump up and attack her as if the ropes around his arms and legs were nothing but strands of thread.

"Shadow Walker is no warrior," the Indian explained. "No more than a wolf or a bear is a warrior. Like those animals, he is a killer. Unlike those animals, he doesn't kill for food or survival. He kills to kill. I know because I've seen it."

"Now that we're all good and scared," Clint said, "you can tell us where to find him."

The Indian looked over to Clint and gave him a smile. For a moment, it seemed he was going to turn mute again. He did eventually start speaking, however. When he did, words tumbled out of him like tepid water dripping from a spout.

"From here, you'll ride north," the Indian said. "You'll ride just into the Crow's land, where you'll find a small village where the Koko people live. From there, you go west toward the hills and where the trees become thick.

"Within those trees, there is a narrow path leading to a river and the base of a larger hill. Along that hill, there will be a camp made of cabins and teepees leading up to where Shadow Walker lives."

"Is he headed there already?"

The Indian shook his head slowly. "He still has some stops to make, so you should be able to find him."

Clint's eyes narrowed as he searched the Indian's face for any sign that he was lying. But as far as he could tell, the Indian wasn't trying to hide anything. Then again, the Indian had yet to break a sweat after the fight, seeing his partner killed and waking up as a prisoner.

"You follow what I say and you'll see Shadow Walker for yourself. I hope you find him. I hope more that I am there when you do."

"Why's that?"

"Because then I could watch as you are torn apart like a fresh deer carcass and fed to his dogs . . . just like the others who have come for him."

TWENTY-FOUR

Clint and Rachel stepped out of the livery and into the darkened fort. Behind them, they left the big Indian tied up, blindfolded and gagged. Although most of the noise had settled down in the saloon and cathouse, things looked pretty much the same as when they'd first seen the two Indians approach them.

Rachel looked behind her and waited a few more steps before saying anything. "Why did you tell him he'd been knocked out so long? We were barely able to get him tied up before he opened his eyes again."

"Most men tend to have fewer qualms about turning in their friends if they think they were left behind by them. At the very least, I figured it would put him off his game a bit."

"Do you think it worked?"

Looking over his shoulder as if he could see through walls and study the Indian inside the livery, Clint replied, "Not really, no."

"Then it was just a waste of time."

"Have you always been so impatient?" Clint asked.

"Only when someone's life is in the hands of a blood-thirsty killer."

Clint stopped and looked around to make sure nobody was watching them or listening to what they were saying. Apart from a few stumbling drunks in the distance and a single, bored man in uniform at the front gate, they were completely alone.

"This was anything but a waste," Clint told her. "How can you even think that when we found out where Coltraine is headed?"

"And you think you can believe that nonsense?"

"I believe that Indian back there truly thinks we'll be killed on our way to the camp or soon after we get there. Besides, I'm not going to take him as my only source of information. It's just another piece of the big picture and we need to use every single piece we can find."

She began to nod. "I . . . want to come with you."

"We do seem to work pretty well together, but I don't know if you're ready to see this all the way through to the end."

"Why not?" she asked angrily.

"For one thing, your temper damn near got us killed and almost called down the rest of those men over in that building," Clint said while pointing to the smaller structure away from the more social businesses. "It may not be as late as we told that Indian, but those men aren't going to be in there forever. One slip could either call down a whole lot more trouble or scare them off into hiding.

"If Coltraine has been transporting kidnapped women for half as long as folks say he has, he'll know his route like the back of his hand. He'll also know plenty of ways to disappear if he thinks he's being followed."

Rachel's eyes narrowed and she crossed her arms over her chest. "I know that. I'm not stupid."

"You've made it this far, so I give you all the credit you deserve. But from here on, things will only get harder. You'll need more than just tenacity to make it out alive. You need to know when to push your feelings down and when to lie low even though every inch of you will want to fight."

"I can fight as good as any man."

Clint pulled in a breath and forced himself to hold it until the frustration inside of him simmered down a bit. "How many times have you actually seen Coltraine?" he asked once he could keep his voice steady.

After glaring defiantly at him for a second or two, Rachel let out a sigh of her own and lowered her eyes. "Not once."

"Me, either. This might be our first chance and I'd rather not let it pass by while we're standing here arguing. If you want to help, you'll have to realize that I may know a thing or two more about how to go about it."

"And you should realize that I can contribute some things as well. I've been following—"

"That's great," Clint interrupted. "And I want to hear everything you've found out, but it'll have to be later. Right now, we need to get in close to whatever is going on over there and we can't be seen in the process."

For the first time since they'd met, Clint actually saw Rachel give a genuine smile. "I'm pretty good at sneaking."

"And if things go bad, you just follow my lead. All right?"

After thinking it over briefly, she nodded. "All right."

"Now," Clint said as he held out his hand, "I'll need my gun."

Rachel's hand went to the modified Colt stuck under her gun belt. It stayed there for a bit as she pulled in a deep breath. Finally, she removed the gun and held it out to him. It took another second, but she eventually let it pass into Clint's hand.

TWENTY-FIVE

Clint had to give her credit for at least one thing. Rachel certainly was one hell of a good sneak.

After he'd pointed out a good way to get over to the small building where the other new arrivals had gone, Clint let Rachel lead for the rest of the way. She moved like a cat and barely seemed to take up more space than one. Keeping low while almost scampering on all fours, she stayed close to the building until she found a small, unattended window.

Compared to her, Clint felt like he was marching over a field of crackling glass. Just before she'd found her spot, he almost lost sight of her altogether. Even when he got up beside her under that window, he swore she wasn't even moving enough to pull in a breath.

Without saying a word, she pointed up to the window. Clint nodded and watched as she inched her way up to get a look inside. Rachel lifted her face to the glass until the slightest sliver of light from within fell over the top of her head. As if sensing that light on her scalp, she froze and stayed perfectly still.

Clint could hear voices on the other side of the wall and pressed his ear against it. Although he could tell the men inside the building were definitely having an important conversation, he couldn't make out any kinds of details. The only thing he had to go on was the urgency in their voices and the quickness of their speech. Rather than keep trying to test the limits of his hearing, Clint moved around to look on either side of the building to make sure nobody was coming.

The tired soldier was right where he'd been the last time Clint had checked. By the looks of him, the young man in uniform was more concerned with looking like he was awake than actually keeping watch on what was going on around him. As far as that went, there really wasn't much going on.

Since the fort had obviously been handed over to saloon owners, drunks, gamblers and a handful of working girls, the soldier didn't really have any official business to tend to. Clint moved around the building as best he could until he heard the creak of hinges coming from the front door.

Someone stepped out of the small building and quickly shut the door behind him. The man looked to be about the same age as the big Indian that was currently tied up in the abandoned livery. He wasn't as big as Clint's prisoner, but he made up for his lack of muscle by carrying at least three guns strapped to his waist and back.

Clint was crouched with his back to the wall. He leaned out as far as he could, then was forced to brace himself with an outstretched hand. Holding the position wasn't easy, but knowing that one slip would announce his presence to everyone inside was a big incentive to stay put.

The man with the three guns stepped out and looked around. He put a cigarette between his lips, struck a match against the door frame and then lit up. While exhaling a plume of smoke, he looked around slowly. Although his attention was drawn to the saloon at first, he soon began to look over in Clint's direction.

It seemed as if the man could sense Clint's eyes on him.

The more Clint hoped for the man to look away, the more the man's eyes were drawn to him. Soon, Clint felt a knot in his stomach as if a beam of light had suddenly been aimed at him. Gritting his teeth, Clint stayed quiet and didn't move a muscle.

He didn't even creep back around the corner when the man stared straight at him and started walking in that direction.

Less than a quarter of Clint's face was peeking around the corner of the building. His hat was pushed to the back of his head and his feet were firmly planted, but Clint still felt like he was on the verge of stumbling or announcing himself some other way.

Keeping his head in place, Clint reached around to place his hand upon the grip of his Colt. If things turned completely for the worst, he would at least be able to get off the first shot.

The man took another few steps, but his eyes soon began to falter. Clint thought he was being overly hopeful, but he soon realized that the other man had walked through some light spilling out from one of the building's front windows.

The light wasn't enough to cast any shadows, but it was enough of a contrast to the darkness outside that it caused the man's eyes to readjust. After a few annoyed blinks, the man strained to catch sight of what he'd seen before and was unable to find a thing. Swearing under his breath, he turned on the balls of his feet and walked away.

Clint let out a sigh of relief, but quickly sucked it back in again when he saw the man was now headed around the other corner. Even though that wouldn't take him directly to where Clint was huddled, it would still lead around the building to where Rachel was peeking into the back window.

Looking down and sifting through the dirt with his fingers, Clint was able to find a pebble that was just big enough to suit his needs. He picked out a target heading toward the saloon, took aim and whipped the pebble through the air.

Although Clint didn't hear anything, he'd found another pebble and tossed that one as well. This time, he heard a smack followed by a loud string of slurred obscenities.

That sudden break in the silence caught the attention of the man with the three guns. He turned to look, but didn't have eyes sharp enough to pick out the third pebble, which sped through the air to hit its target once more.

This time, the man who'd been hit spun around to angrily look behind him. All he could see through the liquor-soaked haze in his head was the gunman standing outside the small building.

"What the fuck is that?" the drunk hollered.

The armed man stepped forward and said, "Just turn back around and mind your own business."

"What did you say?" the drunk replied as he stomped toward the small building.

The gunman responded by taking the shotgun from his back and walking to meet the drunk halfway.

Clint couldn't have asked for a better result and hurried back around to check on how Rachel was faring.

TWENTY-SIX

Clint rounded the corner and nearly drew his gun out of pure reflex when he saw someone rushing straight at him. He kept his reflexes in check, however, when he caught sight of the blond hair tied behind the other person's head.

"Come on," Rachel whispered as she grabbed Clint's hand and dragged him around the building.

Clint planted his feet and stopped her dead in her tracks once he saw where she was headed. "Not that way," he insisted. "Over here."

Making sure they wouldn't run into the man with the three guns as he made his way back to the building, Clint took Rachel to a thick patch of shadows against the fort's perimeter wall. Once there, they both pressed their backs to the split logs and watched several men emerge from the building.

Clint slid along the wall a ways until he was able to get a better look at all of the men at once.

One of the last to step outside was a squat man in his late forties. Although he had one of the better-kept uniforms of the few soldiers left at the fort, he still looked a long ways from being up to army standards. A pronounced gut hung over his belt and the top two buttons of his shirt were open beneath his wrinkled, dark blue jacket.

". . . stay as long as you like," the man in uniform said as he stepped into the open. "Just keep them women out of sight. I don't want them attracting any undue attention."

Another of the men who'd walked outside wore a wide-brimmed hat hanging from a cord around his neck. Thick, dark hair sprouted in curls from his scalp and a curved mustache covered most of his upper lip. Even from where Clint and Rachel were hiding, the man's demented smile could be seen.

"Don't worry none," the man with the curly hair said. "My girls won't give your whores no competition. I doubt some of 'em even know what it's like to lay with a man."

That caused the man in uniform to raise his eyebrows. "Really? How much are you asking for them?"

"More'n you can afford, Sergeant. That is, unless you want to work out a trade for future services here at your fine outpost."

The sergeant considered that for a moment before finally shaking his head. "I'd better not. I . . . that is, we need all the money we can get."

"That's what I figured. The offer's open, though, and a girl like one of these could turn one hell of a profit if you put her to work."

"Maybe next time."

"All right, then. Have them supplies sent over before the morning. We aim to roll out of here before first light."

The sergeant touched his forehead in a halfhearted salute and watched as the man with the curly hair motioned for the rest of his gang to follow him toward the horses tied near the entrance of the fort.

As they watched, Clint could feel the anger coming off Rachel in waves. The moment he felt her start to move away from the wall, he reached out with one arm to force her back into place.

"Let me go," she hissed. "That's the man we're after."

Keeping his voice down to a whisper, Clint said, "I

agree. He's also got the protection of what passes for soldiers at this fort. These men may not be much by military standards, but they're armed and they'll take commands from that asshole right over there."

"I didn't come all this way to get this close and watch Coltraine leave."

Clint turned to look at her squarely, but didn't relax the arm that was holding her back. "Remember when we agreed to work together?"

"Yes, but—"

"But nothing. If we're to work together, we'll need to trust one another. If not, you can rush off and take your chances with your gun and knife against at least half a dozen men who are armed and looking for trouble."

Rachel looked back and forth from Clint to the men working their way toward their horses. As she watched, the men climbed into their saddles, snapped their reins and rode through the front gates.

"You'd damn well better have something better in mind," she said.

Clint showed her a grin and replied, "Oh, I just might."

TWENTY-SEVEN

Sergeant Bray scratched his chin as he walked into the small building he used as an office. It wasn't much, but it had served him well even when Fort Marsden was in active use. Even then, the fort wasn't anything more than a stopover for army caravans and patrols to rest and replenish their supplies. To some degree, that's all it was now.

Back then, Bray had been in charge of keeping supplies stocked. When he'd gotten a promotion, he thought he might finally get posted somewhere closer to civilization. The fact of the matter was that the army wanted to shift its efforts into more important outposts, but it was too lazy to have Fort Marsden taken down.

Bray's promotion left him sitting behind a desk at the same damned fort. It wasn't long before he allowed the other businesses to move in and set up for a fee and a cut of their profits. What made Sergeant Bray even madder was the fact that the army barely seemed to care, just as long as there were supplies set aside for the handful of men who came though every couple of months. Odds were that those men were on their way to an assignment just as bad as the one Bray was stuck with.

Inside his office, Sergeant Bray had just gotten into his

chair and put his feet on his desk when he was interrupted
by a knock at the door. His first impulse was to close his
eyes and pretend he wasn't there. But the knocks came
back and he realized it was only a pipe dream that he could
truly vanish.

When he opened his eyes again, he was still in his dirty
little office within the dirty little fort. Since things couldn't
get much worse, he grunted for whoever was outside to
come in.

The door swung open and a pretty blonde stumbled inside.

"What the hell?" Bray grunted as he squinted at the new
arrival.

Once the blonde moved in a bit farther, it was obvious
that she wasn't just stumbling. She'd been pushed by the
rough-looking fellow who came in right behind her.

"Who the hell are you?" Bray asked as he swung his
legs down and stood up. "This is an official office, you
know."

"I know," Clint said. "I'm just a little late, is all. This
one here got away."

"What're you talking about?"

"This one," Clint repeated while shaking Rachel's arm
and speaking as if he were trying to teach a dog a new trick,
"got away from me. Just tell me where Coltraine got off to."

"What business is that of yours?"

"I'm riding with him, that's what. This bitch here
slipped loose just as we were headed into the fort and I was
to round her up. It must've taken a little longer than he
thought, because Coltraine ain't nowhere to be found."

Sergeant Bray's face was plump and sour, but his eyes
were taking on more and more of a suspicious glint. "He
didn't mention a thing about this to me."

"Does he tell you everything that happens before and
after we get here?" Clint asked in a voice that was so con-
descending he almost wanted to crack himself in the face.

While most men would have let Clint know right then and there how little they appreciated being talked to like an idiotic child, Sergeant Bray was used to it. In fact, he even relaxed a bit when he heard that tone in Clint's voice.

"He doesn't tell me everything," Bray groused, "but he also didn't tell me he was short any men." Eyeing Rachel carefully, he added, "Or women."

"Well, I've barely even seen him lately. Me and this pretty little lady have been escorting a pair of Indians. Perhaps you've seen them. One was a big fella with a knife as long as your arm and the other was carrying a pistol."

Bray nodded. "Yeah, I did see them two." He squinted at Clint for a few seconds before adding, "Come to think of it, I may have seen you before. Sorry about all of this. It's been a long day."

"Hey, don't mention it. I usually get to travel with a whole cartload of fresh girls, but today I get to chase this one instead. I only hope she's worth the trouble I went through to get her back."

"Where are them two Injuns?" Bray asked.

"They're waiting for me outside. I had to separate them from the missus here, before they spoiled the merchandise. I just needed to stop by here and find out where Coltraine's going from here."

Bray stopped and looked at Clint as if he'd suddenly noticed a snout in the middle of his face. His mouth hung open and he blinked slowly while asking, "Didn't you travel with Coltraine all the way here?"

"Yes, but we got separated. Weren't you listening?"

"I was, but . . ."

"Coltraine rides real careful and he doesn't tell the rest of us where we're going until we're almost there. I know we'll end up north, but it's just not safe to plan on every camp until we know it's clear."

Still looking dumbly at Clint, Bray took the opportunity

to glance longingly at Rachel. He let his eyes wander over the front of her body and he didn't try to hide it when they lingered in the vicinity of her chest. In fact, she'd even pulled open a button or two to make certain some attention would be pulled to that area.

Clint snapped his fingers and added more of an edge to his voice when he said, "If you don't want to help, I'll be sure to let Coltraine know about it when I see him."

"He said him and his men were camped about a mile east of here," Bray said. "I didn't ask for any more than that."

"There now," Clint said with a grin, "that wasn't so hard."

Rachel allowed Clint to grab her by the arm and shove her out the door. Even though he was the one handling her, it was all she could do to keep from hauling off and beating the tar out of Sergeant Bray. She could even feel the fat man's eyes on her after she was outside and the door was shut behind her.

"Come on," she said as she pulled free of Clint and stormed toward the main livery. "I have to get the hell out of this place."

TWENTY-EIGHT

Clint and Rachel rode from the fort and headed east. Although it would have been helpful to get more specific directions, Clint had no trouble believing that Coltraine hadn't given any to Sergeant Bray. As anxious as Rachel was to go and question the Indian in the abandoned livery for a while longer, Clint knew that would have been useless as well. In fact, the Indian would likely send them into a trap or, at the least, on a wild-goose chase.

Having a single point on the compass to steer by might not have been much, but it was all they had and more than they'd gotten before. Another factor that seemed to work against them was the darkness itself.

By the time Clint and Rachel left the fort, it was creeping into the early morning hours. As such, every shadow seemed as cold and deep as an underground lake. But it also made it fairly easy to spot campfires from a good distance away.

When Clint saw the first hint of firelight in the distance, he motioned for Rachel to slow down. She did so reluctantly and fidgeted impatiently while Clint took the spyglass from his saddlebag.

"What do you see?" she asked. "Is it them?"

"Give me a second and I'll tell you," Clint replied as he peered through the lenses.

After a couple more seconds, he lowered the spyglass and dropped it back into his bag.

"Well?" Rachel asked.

"It's a camp, all right. A big one."

"That's it?"

"What do you expect me to see? A giant sign painted on the side of a barn telling us that's the place we want?"

Rachel nodded and took a breath to calm herself. "Sorry. It's just that it feels like I've been doing this for a long time and this is the closest I've ever gotten."

"I know the feeling. Still, we can't rush in too quickly or we'll just ruin everything we've done so far."

"But we know where they're headed."

"And that might change if things get too bad," Clint said. "If we step too far in the wrong direction, there's any number of ways these men can get away from us. Or they might not get away from us, but stampede over our bodies instead."

"So what do we do then?"

"We're still headed over there," Clint told her, "but we just need to be quiet about it."

Clint crept toward the camp, hunkered down so low that he was practically crawling. He could hear movement all around him as small groups of men sat around the two fires that had been built, smoking cigars and drinking whiskey. The smell of food still lingered in the air, but it wasn't very appetizing.

As he moved forward, Clint never stopped thinking about the woman he'd left behind. Rachel had a rifle of her own and she was supposed to stay behind that rifle so she could cover Clint if he needed to get back to the horses in a rush. Although she'd agreed to the task, there had been an anxiousness in her eyes that made Clint worry. Then again,

that anxiousness had been there since the first time he'd
seen her.

Clint was soon able to get close enough to listen in on
the conversations taking place around those campfires. By
this time, he was crawling on his belly through the dirt and
bushes like a snake. He made sure his feet, stomach, chest
and chin were all against the ground. It might have been
uncomfortable as hell, but it allowed him to get even closer
to the camp.

The voices he heard were talking about the same sort of
nonsense that would be expected in any group of cowboys.
They lied about women they'd bedded, bragged about
fights they'd been in and gave each other no end of grief.

Clint was beginning to think he was sneaking up on the
wrong camp entirely when he heard a familiar voice come
from one of the tents.

"And that's the reason they ain't here," the voice said.

There was laughter from a couple different sources, but
the man who'd spoken last stepped outside and took a swig
from a bottle in his hand. He was the same man with the
curly hair who had been at Fort Marsden earlier that night.

Clint pressed himself even lower against the ground to
make sure he wouldn't be spotted. It didn't take long to realize none of the men were looking for intruders. On the
contrary, they joked and drank as if they were having a
party.

Since he couldn't make out much of what was being
said between the men anyhow, Clint eased away from the
camp so he could circle around from another angle. He was
able to creep in fairly close no matter what angle he chose
and it wasn't long before he was on his way back to the
spot where he'd left Rachel.

The farther from the camp he went, the more Clint allowed himself to walk upright. When his back was almost
straightened completely, he stopped and squinted into the
shadows as a chill worked its way under his skin.

Rachel wasn't where he'd left her.

Just to be certain, Clint kept moving until he found Eclipse standing right next to what should be Rachel's horse. He worked his way back and wound up in the same spot as before. The spot was still empty.

Trying to figure out where he should look for her first, Clint turned around and nearly jumped out of his skin when he saw Rachel crouched nearby with the rifle pointed at him.

As soon as she saw his face, she lowered the gun and said, "I told you I was good at sneaking."

"You sure did. Let's get moving."

"What about the prisoners? When do we come back for them?"

"Not for a while," Clint explained. "They're not here."

TWENTY-NINE

"What do you mean they're not here?" Rachel asked. "Where are they?"

"I don't know. What I do know is that we were real lucky to have gotten this far without being seen. How about we discuss this somewhere else instead of pushing our luck?"

Rachel had a hold on her saddle horn, but was still looking in the direction of the camp. When she pulled herself up, she practically jumped onto the horse's back and kept her eyes fixed upon the spot that Clint had just explored.

"Hold on now," Clint said as he reached out to grab hold of Rachel's reins.

She snapped her head toward him and spoke through gritted teeth. "Let go of those."

"What do you think you're doing?"

"I'm going after those men. Or are you telling me that they're not there either?"

"They were there, but you didn't give me a chance to tell you much of anything, did you?"

"All right, then. Tell me."

"Not here. Every word we say right now is just making that much more noise. We're leaving."

Rather than wait for agreement or possibly another fight, Clint got Eclipse moving away from the camp without letting go of Rachel's reins. Her horse came along much more willingly than she did and soon they had put some distance between themselves and the camp.

Once the walls of Fort Marsden could be seen again as a black shape in the distance, Rachel pulled back her reins and brought her horse to a stop.

Clint felt the leather straps slip through his fingers and immediately brought Eclipse around to face her. "Charging in there isn't the way to go about it," Clint said before she could start unleashing whatever was on the tip of her tongue.

Amazingly enough, she nodded in agreement. "I know. I just don't want to get too far away from them."

Picking up on the calmness that had slipped into her voice, Clint eased up next to her and said, "There's a good amount of men in that camp. Enough that they won't be able to go anywhere without leaving that sign I mentioned not too long ago."

"You can track them?" Rachel asked.

"Now that I know where to start and what I'm looking for? Yeah. I should be able to track them."

Even though she was still nodding, Rachel's eyes were darting back and forth as if trying to follow one leaf in the middle of a windstorm. "But those prisoners have got to be close. If they're not at the camp, they've got to be—"

"I know," Clint interrupted. "Believe me, I've had plenty of time to think about all of this. I had to stop because my head's starting to feel like it's full of smoke. I'm dead tired and you must be, too."

"There'll be plenty of time to sleep later."

"Or we could always fall out of our saddles somewhere

along the way. Neither one of us knows how these men travel, but we do know they're camped out right now. That's a real good time for us to rest before things get too crazy again."

Slowly, Rachel's eyes lost their momentum and began settling into the bottom of their sockets. Once she was looking down at her horse's neck, she let out a breath that sounded as if she'd been holding it for several days.

"It has been a long time since I've slept for more than a minute or two," she admitted.

"Me, too."

Clint and Rachel wound up at a nice spot between Fort Marsden and the camp they'd discovered. From there, Clint knew he could keep an eye on both locations, with a minimum amount of places where anyone could slip through without being seen. They built no fire, which didn't affect them too much anyway since neither of them were very hungry.

After sharing some bread and cold bacon, Clint sat up to keep watch while Rachel curled up in her bedroll. Clint's spyglass was never out of reach and his own rifle was propped nearby just in case a target presented itself outside of his Colt's range.

"Why are you doing this?" Rachel asked in a voice that was so soft it seemed more like a trick of the breeze.

"A young girl was taken from Markton," Clint replied.

"I've never been there. Who was she?"

"Someone's sister. Someone who didn't deserve to be stolen like some thing that had been left outside for too long."

Rachel was lying on her side, so she propped up her head on one arm. "I meant who was she to you?"

"I guess she wasn't really close to me. I might have met her once."

"And you're going through all this trouble to help her?"

Clint nodded. "That's right."

"Why?"

"Because nobody else was going to."

"That's a noble thing."

Chuckling to himself, Clint said, "You make it sound like a bad joke."

"That's just because I don't see many noble things," Rachel replied. "Usually, it's just a way for men to put a friendly face onto whatever shit they really want to do."

Hearing Rachel talk was a strange thing. Her voice was soft and smooth, but it also sounded perfectly comfortable tossing out obscenities or demanding a fight with a gang of kidnappers. In a way, her voice matched the rest of her. As she lay there with her bedroll revealing more than half of her body, she made no effort to cover herself up.

She'd stripped down to her shirt, which served as a small nightgown. Even so, the lithe curves of her body were plain enough to be seen. Her muscles shifted like a cat's beneath her skin, making it seem like she was a second away from pouncing.

"My sister was taken by those bastards, too," she said.

"What's her name?"

"Emily." Saying that word changed Rachel completely. It seemed to warm her from the inside for a few seconds. Once those seconds had passed, her edge resurfaced. "She took off to work in Silver City and never came home. I was there covering the same old ground when I stumbled upon you."

Clint took a moment to think back to his time in Silver City. He tried to remember the faces he'd seen on the street and the women he'd seen at the Peacock's Feather, but couldn't recall so much as a glimpse of Rachel. Of course, considering how well she slipped through the shadows, that wasn't too surprising.

"I've heard so much about Coltraine," she said, "but I really don't know anything. He's like a damned ghost."

"Shadow Walker," Clint said. "That's what the Indians call him."

Rachel shut her eyes, flipped onto her other side and grunted, "Soon they'll just call him dead."

THIRTY

Clint woke up early the next morning with a rock jabbing into the base of his spine. His bedroll was wrapped around him as if he needed any more proof of how roughly he'd slept. The few hours of rest that he'd gotten was all right, but he'd felt more comfortable before he allowed Rachel to take her turn watching their camp.

Shifting so the rock was no longer digging into him, Clint rubbed his eyes and tried to look past the aching of his muscles. He quickly gave that up as a lost cause and started looking around for Rachel. He found her at the edge of the camp, changing into a fresh set of clothes. Clint didn't intentionally sneak a look at her as she stripped down and tossed her old clothes aside, but he wasn't about to look away either.

Her body was even more trim that he'd guessed. Her stomach was defined by smooth lines of muscle that led all the way down to a tight little backside. She had her fresh clothes ready, so she was only naked for a second, but it was a second worth savoring. Rachel's breasts were pert and small, but still rounded enough to be a pretty sight. Her little nipples were erect in the cool morning air and poked from behind the thin layer of cotton that was the undershirt she pulled on over her head.

After wriggling into her jeans and buckling her belt, she strapped her holster around her waist and bent down to pick up her hat. She placed the hat upon her head and reached behind her to gather up the blond tangles of her hair.

"Enjoying yourself?" she asked without looking over her shoulder at Clint.

Suddenly, Clint felt like a boy who'd been caught hiding behind a bush at the girls' swimming hole. He laughed that off and shrugged after sitting up. "Actually, I'd be lying if I said anything but yes."

"And I'd be insulted if you did."

"Did I miss any excitement while I was asleep?"

"I saw a nice bunch of hawks fly overhead, but that's about it."

Clint gathered up his bedroll and stuffed it in its place on his saddle. When he saw Rachel watching him, he asked, "I can change my clothes, too, if you want a show for yourself."

She laughed and shook her head. "Right now, I'd settle for something to eat."

"Here," Clint said as he dug some beef jerky from his saddlebag and tossed it to her. "Save some for me. I'm going to check on that camp."

"Bring it along. I'm coming with you."

Clint would have also been lying if he'd told her he wasn't expecting that. Rather than try to argue, he finished gathering up his things and strapped the saddle onto Eclipse's back. The Darley Arabian was quicker to wake up than he was and was ready for a morning run. He got just that as Clint and Rachel raced back to Coltraine's camp.

Before charging straight through the trees that he'd crawled through the night before, Clint steered Eclipse around them so he could get a better look. It wasn't so much of a forest as it was a large cluster of greenery made up of some middle-aged trees surrounded by dense bushes.

Since there wasn't much to see around the perimeter of those trees, Clint led the way back into them. He and Rachel pulled back their reins once they were in the same spot where they'd left the horses before and Clint dropped down into his familiar crouch.

"Be right back," he whispered.

Rachel nodded, but remained in her saddle.

Clint started at a brisk pace, but moved even faster once he caught the distinct odor of smoke. The smell was more powerful than it had been the night before, which told him the fires had been doused not long ago. Feeling a sense of urgency flood through him, Clint allowed himself to move at a quicker, loping pace.

There were no voices drifting through the air.

There were no sounds of horses or of supplies being packed away.

As Clint moved forward toward the clearing where the fires had been built, he found nothing.

"Jesus," he muttered as he stood in his spot and looked around. Clint thought back to make sure he'd returned to the right place. He looked at the trees surrounding him and even the horizon so he could compare it to what he'd seen before.

He was definitely in the same spot. Now, the only question that remained was if he'd dreamed the camp had been there the night before.

Just to be certain, Clint circled the area and looked around for any hints that had been left behind. With the sun beaming through the trees and not a cloud in the sky, searching the area was a whole lot easier than it had been previously. Of course, that made it even more frustrating when Clint came up short.

Clint stepped back into the clearing and took another look. He went to the places where the tents had been and couldn't find so much as a hole in the ground where a stake had been driven. He couldn't find any footprints in the dirt where he knew all those men had walked. He couldn't even find a single bit of trash that had been tossed aside or left behind.

Not one cigarette butt.

Not a scrap of food.

Not one damn thing.

Finally, Clint thought back to what he'd seen the night before and narrowed down the exact spot where the campfires had been built. He squatted down and used his bare hands to dig in the dirt. At first, he felt like a crazy man who'd convinced himself he was a dog. When his fingers sifted through nothing but more dirt and the occasional rock, he felt like he was losing his mind.

When he finally did touch something that hadn't grown there naturally, Clint only felt slightly better.

He pulled his hand from the dirt and examined the one thing he had to show for all his efforts. It was half of a matchstick. Clint took that little sliver of wood back to Rachel and showed it to her after climbing onto Eclipse's back.

"What's that?" she asked.

"This," Clint replied solemnly, "is why Coltraine's called Shadow Walker. Tracking him is going to be a lot harder than I thought."

THIRTY-ONE

They rode back to Fort Marsden as if they were in a race. Clint and Rachel bolted through the gates, jumped from their saddles and marched straight toward Sergeant Bray's small quarters. Before they got to the door, however, Clint stopped and wheeled around to face Rachel.

"Let me go in alone," he said.

"If this is about a man being able to get farther than a woman, I swear I'll smack you, Clint."

"That's exactly what this is about, but not from me. Did that sergeant strike you as willing to listen to reason where you were concerned?"

All Rachel had to do was start to think about the way Bray had stared at her without even caring whether or not she caught him doing it and she got Clint's point. She also got a creepy chill running along her back.

"I'm not going to just stand here and wait, though," she said.

"I hope not. See what you can find from the businessmen around here. They're the ones who seem to know more about Coltraine's comings and goings than anyone else." Clint's next impulse was to make sure she would be ready if she stumbled upon someone who didn't want to be found. Seeing her in front of him with her gun at her side and that fire in her eyes, Clint had to wonder if any of those kidnappers would be prepared if they stumbled upon her.

"I'll check around," she said. "Let's just hope that the sergeant is still somewhere you can find him."

"He didn't strike me as the sort who would go anywhere."

Rachel had started to walk away when she felt Clint grab her wrist. She turned around, and saw his eyes drift down to her waist.

"You might want to cover up that gun," he said. "Folks might be a little friendlier to you that way."

Pulling out the tails of her shirt, she draped them over her holster. It wouldn't hold up to close inspection, but it was enough to keep the firearm out of sight. Once that was done, Rachel hurried off toward the saloon.

Clint stood there and watched her until he could swear *he* was being observed. Actually, he waited until the guards who were supposed to be watching everyone started paying attention to him instead of whatever had occupied their minds before. When the uniformed men started looking his way, Clint ignored them and headed into Sergeant Bray's office.

The sergeant was sitting in the same spot he'd been the night before. His uniform was a little more rumpled and the odor coming from the fat disgrace wearing those colors was a little more pungent.

"Hello again, Sergeant," Clint said. "I see you haven't freshened up since the last time we met. That's just plain sad since I slept outside and you've got a whole fort."

"Who the hell are you?" the sergeant asked groggily.

Clint bypassed any more formalities by stepping around Bray's desk and grabbing the sergeant by his already rumpled collar. "I'm the one who needs to know some more information about Coltraine."

For a few seconds, Bray kept staring at Clint as if he were still trying to place his face. Suddenly, his eyes lit up a bit and he asked, "Didn't you catch up to him yet?"

"Not yet. Where should I look?"

"You can start by looking behind you."

Clint turned to do just that. Instead of Coltraine, he found one of the younger men in uniform standing in the back of the room holding a rifle at the ready. The rifle's barrel was pointed directly at Clint's chest.

Settling Bray down, Clint straightened up and tried to get himself in a better position. He was surprised to make it so that his back was mostly to a wall and both of the other men were in his line of sight.

Sergeant Bray got up and tugged at his jacket as if that little bit of effort would make one bit of difference. "What you and the rest of your pimp friends don't realize is that I am an officer in the United States Army. As such, I am not to be treated like the civilians at this fort."

Standing up as though he were posing for a picture, Bray announced, "I could have you shot for what you've done just now."

"Sure you could," Clint said with a nod. "And I could have you court-martialed for what you've been allowing to happen at this fort. I understand the army doesn't exactly need this place anymore, but I doubt the men higher up on the chain of command know the full extent of your business ventures."

Bray's mouth tightened into a straight line. "You won't be able to report a damn thing if you don't make it out of this office."

Clint stood up tall and let his hand hover over his holstered Colt. "Easier said than done, Sergeant."

The next couple of seconds dragged on like hours. Clint kept his eye mainly on the soldier with the rifle, but he also wasn't about to take his sights off of Bray for too long.

The soldier was a young recruit who looked like he'd barely made it through basic training. He held onto his rifle as if he were praying to the Lord above that the weapon wouldn't have to be used as anything more than a threat.

Bray, himself, did a fairly good job of maintaining his composure. At least, he maintained it right until he let out his next breath.

"I don't know a damn thing more about Coltraine, all right?" Bray sputtered.

"Where did he go from here?"

"Probably Norwalk. That's where he always heads when he's making his rounds."

Clint thought for a few moments and then remembered visiting Norwalk once or twice the last time he'd been in this part of the country. It was a dusty little town without much more than a few saloons and a good spot along the river in its favor. "When's he due back?" he asked.

"Not for another couple of days, and that's just to pick up the man he left behind. Our business is done and he won't want to talk to me until next time. Otherwise, he'll only get suspicious."

"What man did he leave behind?"

THIRTY-TWO

Clint walked out of the little building to find Rachel standing not too far away with her arms crossed. The moment she saw him, she walked forward wearing a look on her face that made it obvious just how anxious she was to ask her next question.

"What did he say?"

"He said we've got half an hour to get out of this fort before he puts us in the stockade," Clint replied. "But that should be more than enough time for us to pay a visit to the man who's staying at the cathouse."

"What man?"

Clint smirked and started walking toward the block-shaped building. "The man Coltraine left behind to scout for prospects. He'll pick out a woman or two who will accompany him and Coltraine north when he gets back from Norwalk."

"You know all this for certain?" she asked.

"If we manage to catch up to Coltraine and things go our way, the sergeant will be out some money, but he won't be forced to hand over the girls working here every now and then. From what I've gathered, these soldiers are just too lazy to do anything but pay whatever Coltraine demands.

"If Coltraine comes out ahead in this," Clint continued, "then things are back where they were and the sergeant can just take credit for delivering us to Coltraine's men. Either way, he doesn't stand to lose much. Besides, the man's too lazy to fight Coltraine and he's too lazy to stand up to us."

"You were busy in there," she said.

"I think Coltraine's been crossing the line by treating this fort like it was his own. Apparently, the sergeant doesn't like playing host to those Indians and he sure as hell doesn't appreciate hosting one of Coltraine's men just so he can have his pick of the litter in that cathouse."

"Coltraine doesn't just do that here," Rachel said grimly. "He always makes sure he gets someone he wants in these deals. He sure took his time in selecting my sister."

"Well, the only thing this fellow will be doing is getting us close to Coltraine."

Suddenly, Rachel looked over to Clint and said, "Coltraine never got a look at me."

"That's . . . good."

"What I mean is that he wouldn't recognize me," she added quickly. "Neither would his men. I'm sure the women at this cathouse would have no problem letting me in as one of their own so I could get in good with the asshole who's over there now."

Shaking his head, Clint said, "Absolutely not! That's too big of a risk. Coltraine is going to be hard enough to find and there's already too many innocent lives at stake. I don't want to gamble yours as well."

"It won't be a gamble. It'll be a safer bet, if anything else. I'll make sure I get picked and I can make it easier for you to follow us straight to him and the rest of them. As it is, we might not be able to find Coltraine anyhow. You said it yourself that he didn't even leave a useful track at that camp."

"No," Clint said firmly. "You're not going to convince me this is a good idea."

"It may just be the only idea that can work. There's not much time left and God only knows what Coltraine is doing right now!"

"And you won't be able to help anyone if you're dead," Clint said. "Which is what you'll be the moment Coltraine or anyone else suspects you're trying to pull something over on them."

Letting out a sigh, Rachel said, "All right."

"Good," Clint said as he stepped closer to her. Even though there weren't a lot of people around at the moment, he lowered his voice so only she could hear him. "We can do this, but we just need to be smart about it."

"I know."

Clint wasn't entirely convinced that she could be dissuaded so easily, but he saw that she was at least willing to listen to him. "Did you find anything interesting while I was being threatened by the army?"

"Remember that Indian we left tied up in the livery?"

"Yeah."

"He's still in there."

"Jesus," Clint groaned. "These soldiers are even lazier than I thought."

"I'm not even sure they found him yet," Rachel said. "He looked like he was asleep, but he might almost be through his ropes. I'll need your help to get him tied up again before he gets loose."

"As much as I'd like to see how the sergeant deals with that Indian when he gets free," Clint said as he turned toward the small, nearly empty building that had once been a second livery, "that would only give him something else to leverage against us."

Clint stopped inside the doorway of the abandoned livery and fixed his eyes upon the large shape lying on the floor. He couldn't tell if the Indian was unconscious and before he could ask, he felt a sharp blow to the back of his head.

Holding her gun by the barrel, Rachel stood behind Clint and waited to see if she would have to hit him again. Although he wavered and started to turn around, Clint dropped to his knees and fell into a pile of hay on the floor. His hand was already wrapped around his modified Colt.

Rachel flipped the gun around so she was holding it properly and walked over to where the big Indian was lying. He truly had been about to break out of his ropes when she'd found him, but hadn't been able to free himself before she'd arrived.

"Who's coming to help you?" she asked.

The Indian stared defiantly at the opposite wall. "I need nobody's help."

"So nobody knows you're here?"

He shrugged as best he could considering how he was tied.

Rachel holstered her gun and carefully drew the knife from its scabbard on her boot. As she lowered herself to one knee, she could see nearly every muscle in the Indian's body tense. That, alone, was enough for her to see that he'd loosened the ropes a bit more than she'd guessed.

"If I let you go, I want you to tell me a good way to get close to Coltraine," she said.

The Indian gazed up at her with large, dark eyes. After contemplating for a moment, he nodded. "I can give you some help in return for my freedom."

"I thought you might prefer a fair trade to threats."

"You are a smart woman," the Indian said with a grin.

Rachel moved slowly toward the Indian. The closer she got, the more relaxed he became until he turned and rolled onto his side to give her a better view of the ropes tying his arms and legs.

Once she was close enough, Rachel buried the knife into the Indian's back.

The big man flailed and started to kick, but was unable to dislodge the knife or Rachel from his back. In fact, his movements only drove the knife in deeper as it was pulled at an awkward angle through his flesh.

Feeling her grip starting to falter, Rachel knew she wouldn't have been able to get this far if the Indian hadn't shown her his back. As she hung on and tried to do as much damage as she could, she thought back to what Clint had said about keeping quiet before more trouble landed on their shoulders.

Even though that made perfect sense, she still doubted her choice of the knife over the gun when it came to putting the Indian in his grave. But even if the Indian managed to take her with him, she would never regret her decision to kill him.

The world was better off without one more animal like him in it.

Before too much longer, the Indian's struggles eased up. His arms stopped straining against the ropes even as one of them snapped under the pressure. Finally, his legs slackened and his body slumped until he was totally limp.

Rachel was breathing heavily and couldn't move her leg. Before she panicked, she realized the Indian was merely lying on her left foot. It came free with a bit of tugging, allowing her to scramble to one side. She grabbed the knife but had to fight to pull it from the Indian's back. Her instincts told her to stab him again just to be sure he was dead, but she couldn't muster up the strength to follow through.

When she got to her feet, she felt like she was going to be sick. Rachel managed to fight back the urge to vomit as she turned her back to the corpse and headed for the door.

As much as she wanted to apologize to Clint, Rachel knew she'd have a chance to do that later. At least, she prayed Clint would be able to track her down so she could see him again. If not, all of this would be for nothing.

THIRTY-THREE

Rachel walked into the building that had once been the fort's bunkhouse. Even though it had been decorated a bit to hide its military roots, the army influence was still there, making the place seem like a shoddy attempt to dress a pig.

The moment she stepped inside, she saw several sets of eyes turn in her direction. Most of those were women who lounged about, waiting to pounce on any man who glanced their way. But there was also a man leaning against a wall, bracing himself with one arm in a way that kept a small blonde from escaping him. That man looked over at Rachel without trying to hide the lust in his eyes.

Rachel put a friendly smile on her face and walked into the next room.

"Excuse me," a short woman with brown hair said. "Can I help you with something?"

Rachel kept moving until she knew she was out of the man's sight. Before the other woman could say anything else, Rachel looked at her and nodded. "Yes. Actually, I think I might be able to help you with something."

The other woman allowed her long brown hair to flow over her shoulders. There was a natural curliness to her hair that made it seem more like liquid. Her skin was pale and her nose was slightly bulbous, but she was far from un-attractive. She looked at Rachel with suspicion at first, but then shook her head. "If you're looking for work, you should look somewhere else," she said.

"I don't intend on taking a job."

"Then what do you want?"

Before she continued talking, Rachel reached behind her to close the door.

The other woman took notice of that immediately. She also noticed the gun on Rachel's hip. "There's hardly any money here," she said. "All of it's collected every morning by—"

"I'm not here for money. What's your name?"

"Jennifer."

"Mine's Rachel. I'm here about the man who's waiting here for Coltraine."

"I . . . don't . . . I really shouldn't talk about him."

"I'm trying to get close to those bastards and give them what they've got coming before any more women are kidnapped and sold off like property."

"What do you know about that?"

"My sister was taken," Rachel explained. "She was picked out and handed over just like so many others. Just like one of your girls is going to be when Coltraine comes back."

Jennifer slowly shook her head. "Sometimes they take one of my girls with them, but they're just going to work somewhere else. Sometimes, it's either that or lose your job altogether. That's why they usually pick the ones who don't have any ties around here."

"This is a whorehouse in an old army fort," Rachel said harshly. "Even the damn army doesn't have ties here anymore." She pulled in a calming breath and looked Jennifer in the eyes. "Look, whatever you were told about this, it's a lie. It's one of the lies that these men always tell so they can get these women to go along as quietly as they can. You can't believe this line of bull."

Jennifer had remained steady at first, but slowly lowered her eyes. "I never knew Coltraine went to more places than this and a house in Norwalk."

"He's got a whole circuit worked out where he's got men who'll hand over women in return for money. That's all it is to these bastards."

"I used to work at a place in California," Jennifer said. "Where we used to get a say in who we took upstairs and even what we charged. Other places are rougher, but this . . . this is a place I've been trying to leave for a while."

"You wouldn't want to leave with animals like that one out there still doing what they're doing."

"No," Jennifer said. "I wouldn't."

"And you've got to believe me when I tell you I know for a fact what they're doing."

Jennifer nodded weakly. "I believe you."

"Then let me try to do something about it."

"Sergeant Bray won't take a stand against them and I won't put my girls in any more danger than they already are."

"I'm not asking you to fight them," Rachel said.

"Then what is it you want from me?"

THIRTY-FOUR

"Mr. Rice?" Jennifer said as she stepped up to where the man was still leaning against the wall.

The man turned toward her slowly, as if he was hesitant to take his eyes from the woman he had trapped in a corner. Once he got a look at Jennifer, however, he took his arm back and shifted so he used his body to trap the other woman instead.

"Hello there," Rice said.

Jennifer put on an empty smile and stepped aside so the woman behind her could be seen. "I'd like to introduce someone to you."

"I was getting along quite well with this little lady," he replied.

"But I think you might want to spend a few moments with this one. Her name is . . ."

Before the pause could seem too long, Rachel stepped forward and extended her hand. "You can call me Lilly."

Rice's lips curled up into a wide smile to display a crooked set of stained teeth. He nodded slowly as he let his eyes take in every last inch of her.

Rachel wore a dark red dress that had been borrowed from one of the many closets inside the converted bunk-

135

house. It didn't fit her perfectly, but the fact that it was a bit too small only made it that much more effective. The waist pulled in to show the curve of her hips, while the top clung to her breasts like a second skin. When she held out an arm to shake Rice's hand, the buttons on the front of the dress strained just a bit.

"My, my," Rice said. "What a lovely name. What a lovely girl."

"Thank you."

Jennifer kept her eyes on the other woman who Rice had trapped in the corner. "It's all right, honey," she said. "I think Mr. Rice and Lilly would like to get to know each other."

The third woman of the group looked confused by Rachel, but took comfort from the fact that Jennifer seemed to be vouching for the new arrival. She moved reluctantly at first, but when she realized that Rice was really going to let her go, the woman was more than happy to get away.

"Is there anything I can get you?" Jennifer asked.

Rice didn't take his eyes off of the smooth contours of Rachel's cleavage when he replied, "Maybe someplace nice and quiet where me and Lilly here can . . . talk."

When Jennifer looked at Rachel, she made certain her meaning was clear as she said, "If you need anything at all, you just holler for me."

Rachel smiled. "I think I can handle this one."

Reluctantly, Jennifer walked away to leave them alone.

Repositioning his arm so it now blocked Rachel in, Rice leaned forward and pulled in a long, noisy breath. "You smell real good."

"Thank you."

"You know who I am?"

"I was told that you're real important and that you're here to get a look at the best this place has to offer." Reaching out to slide her hand along Rice's chest, she added, "If she told me how handsome you were, I wouldn't have taken so long to get here."

Rice's smile remained in place as if it had been painted there. He kept nodding as if his head were attached to a rusty spring. "You like workin' here?"

"It's all right."

"You must be new. I would'a remembered a fine thing like yourself from the last time I came callin'."

"I just got here from back East. New York, to be exact." As she said that, Rachel gambled that Rice hadn't even seen pictures of New York. Judging by the blank look on his face, she'd made a safe bet.

"You know who I work for?"

Rachel furrowed her brow and kept playing with Rice's lapel. "You're not the boss?"

"That'd be a man by the name of Coltraine. He runs one of the finest places in the country. Only the best poker games are played there. Only the best food and only the best women. That'd be where you come in."

Rachel had to fight to keep nodding and smiling as she heard that. Inside, she was wondering if this was the same line that had been fed to her sister, or if she'd been lured in some other way.

"How much is the pay?" she asked.

"Our girls all leave as wealthy ladies. That's why we want the best. You got many friends or family nearby?"

"No. Why?"

"No reason," Rice said with a wolfish grin. "It just works out better if you're not holding to anyone else. You might be gone a while and you may even want to stay for good. Is there anyone who might want to come along?"

"Would that be a problem?"

"Not at all. You just tell us where to find them and we'll fetch 'em for you. Of course, sometimes they don't want to go and we ain't about to drag them along kicking and screaming."

Still thinking back to when her sister had disappeared, Rachel remembered hearing about two strange men who'd been asking where they could find her. She'd been away at the store at the time and those men never returned.

After all that had happened, Rachel hadn't thought too much about those strangers.

Now, the thought of who those men probably were made her sick.

Rice placed his hand on Rachel's hip and moved it around to her backside. From there, he pulled her in close and said, "But I can't just take you because you look good in that dress. I need to know what I'm gettin'."

"By all means, then," she said as she grabbed his wrist and pulled him toward one of the many small rooms, "let me get you alone so I can show you what I've got."

THIRTY-FIVE

Even though someone had taken the effort to spruce up the front couple of rooms in the bunkhouse, the bedrooms had been left in their original condition. The room that Rachel chose was just big enough to hold the small bed, a smaller table and a single chair.

Rice must have known his way around those rooms pretty well because he stripped off his shirt and draped it over the chair without even looking at what he was doing. His boots were kicked off as well and shoved in the space between the bed and table.

"You're a sight for sore eyes, darlin'," he said. "I thought I was gonna have to choose from one of these sorry excuses that've been workin' here for years."

Doing her best to keep from slapping him, she slowly unbuttoned the top of her dress. Rachel glanced down between Rice's legs and saw he was already hard and waiting for her.

Rice pulled down his pants just enough for him to reach inside and stroke himself. "Sometimes I really love my job," he said. "Time for you to impress me."

Stepping back as if to make sure he could see all of her, Rachel was making more sure that she was out of his arm's reach. Considering the size of the room, that was close to impossible. Once her shoulders bumped against the wall, she leaned against the wooden slats and arched her back.

"Ooo, that's nice," Rice said as he watched her slowly pull open the rest of the buttons and slip the material off her shoulders.

Rachel peeled the top of her dress down and let her fingertips slide against her bare breasts. Closing her eyes, she allowed her own touch to linger on her nipples just long enough for them to grow hard and sensitive. Rachel then rubbed them with her thumb before sliding her hand farther down along her stomach.

When she opened her eyes again, she saw Rice coming toward her with his hand still down the front of his pants. In one swift motion, she raised a leg so that her foot pressed against Rice's chest. That allowed her skirt to fall away and reveal the slender curve of her thigh, while also keeping Rice in his place.

Even though Rice was anxious to get closer, he didn't try too hard to move her leg. Instead, he grabbed hold of it with his free hand and groped up as far as he could reach. All Rachel had to do was lock her knee in order to keep him from getting any higher up her leg than she wanted. Rice seemed to be more than happy to do what he was told. So happy, in fact, that Rachel got an idea that might make everything a whole lot easier to bear.

"I want you to sit down," she said softly.

"Yes ma'am."

Rice did as he was told, like an obedient puppy, and dropped himself down onto the only chair in the room. His eyes were wide and his mouth hung open as if he were seeing something he'd never seen before.

As Rachel eased herself out of her dress, she let her hands glide along her body to slowly trace a line along her bare skin. The dress was tight enough that she had to pull and tug to get it over her hips. When it was only halfway down, she eased her fingers between her legs and arched her back while letting out a trembling sigh.

"Oh, God," she whispered. "You're making me so wet."

Rachel didn't need to open her eyes to know that Rice's excitement was building. She could hear his breathing become quicker until he was practically gasping for air. She could also hear the creaks in the chair as he leaned closer to her.

Turning around sharply, Rachel put her back to him and settled in between his legs. She leaned back even more until her shoulders were grinding against his chest. Pushing up with her legs, she squirmed even more while moving her hand up and down along the front of her body.

As she felt Rice's hand work its way around to her front, she took hold of it and placed it on top of her other hand. "Here," she said. "Feel for yourself."

Even though Rice could only feel the back of her hand, he reacted to the way it moved between her legs. Every so often, he brushed against the silky smooth skin of her inner thigh, which was enough to make him let out a moan of his own.

"You like that?" Rachel asked. "Because I know I do."

"Oh, yeah. Now, I wanna—"

"Don't stop!" she cut in. Arching her back even more, she clenched her legs tightly around her and Rice's hands. She could feel him pull in an excited breath, even though he was now actually farther away from what he wanted to touch.

With her hand keeping him in check, Rachel moaned louder and faster while grinding her tight backside against his groin. In no time at all, she could feel his muscles tensing and his breathing grow as heavy as if he'd run a few miles to get into that room.

After she'd built up enough, Rachel let out a long, trembling sigh and let her legs open once more. "Oh, my God," she gasped. "That was so good."

"Really?"

"Yes. Now, it's your turn."

"Jesus, yes," Rice said in a voice that was tight as a bowstring.

Rachel got to her feet and bent at the waist as she slowly wriggled the rest of the way out of her dress. She exaggerated every movement, making sure to brush against him with her legs or backside whenever possible. On the few occasions that she felt his rigid penis bump against her, she moved away in less than a second. By the time she turned around to face him, Rachel felt as if she were standing in front of a keg of dynamite with a half-inch fuse.

Lowering herself to her knees, she leaned forward and rubbed her breasts against his cock. "Ready?"

"Y-yes!"

Her nipples were hard, but that was mostly due to the way she'd touched herself. Rachel took hold of his penis in one hand and then leaned forward with her mouth open wide. Before placing one lip on him, she reached out to rake her nails against his chest and slide him between her breasts a few more times.

Rice was leaning back in his chair and staring down at her through eyes that were halfway shut. He grabbed her hair and pumped his hips so he could ease back and forth along her chest.

Once she'd had enough of that, Rachel held him back by using one hand pressed against his chest and stroked him with her other hand while bobbing her head up and down.

When she'd started, she thought she might have to put him in her mouth for a little while. Although the thought of that didn't sit right with her, it was much better than the alternative. As it turned out, all she needed to do was keep moving her hand for a little while longer as she bobbed and swayed her head.

Rice was already so worked up that he didn't even notice he hadn't once felt her mouth touch him. He didn't even notice when she moved aside just as he was about to finish.

"That was . . . that was . . ." Rice stammered breathlessly as he cleaned himself off.

The longer it took for him to find his words, the more Rachel worried about what he was going to say.

Finally, he got up, pulled up his pants and shouted, "Hot damn! You're the one I'm takin' with me! I just may even keep you for myself!"

Rachel smiled up at him, but had to struggle to keep from laughing.

THIRTY-SIX

Clint woke up with a splitting headache.

When he reached back to feel the spot that hurt the most, he realized where that headache had come from. His hand touched against a spot that was slick with blood and another jolt of pain lanced through his head. After sucking in a sharp breath, he examined the wound as best he could.

From what he could feel, there was a small gash, plenty of blood and one hell of a bump on his head. It wasn't anything too serious, though, but that didn't make him feel any better. Although it took a few tries for him to get his legs steady beneath him, Clint managed to get up and take a look around.

The livery was just as it had been the last time he'd seen it, except for one difference. The big Indian was lying in a slightly different position and was now in a large pool of blood. Clint walked over to the Indian and only had to look at him for a few seconds to figure out what had happened.

"Jesus Christ, Rachel," he said under his breath. "What have you done?"

The longer Clint stood there, the more things rushed back into his head. For starters, he remembered exactly where he was and who was in charge of the fort. Sergeant Bray wasn't much for ambition, but even he would see the opportunity to nail the murder of the Indian on the man who was found next to the body. Considering how well they got along, Clint didn't really want to be in that spot.

When he saw the body of the other Indian who had been killed in their first fight, Clint was even quicker to get the hell out of there.

Eclipse was standing next to Rachel's horse in the spot where they'd been left earlier. Clint patted the Darley Arabian on the nose as he headed straight for the cathouse. He didn't bother with any formalities as he pushed open the door, stepped inside and started looking around.

The women's faces lit up as they saw him. Several of them walked toward Clint, while others merely positioned themselves so he could get a look at what they had to offer. The first one to make it to him was a petite redhead with pert little breasts.

"Hello there," she said.

Still looking at the rest of the women and then leaning over to try and glance down the hall, Clint asked, "Where's the man Coltraine left behind?"

The redhead scowled a bit and said, "He's gone."

"How long ago?"

"Do you just want to talk?"

"Yes, I—"

"Then talk to Jennie," the redhead said as she stepped aside and pointed toward the woman with the dark, curly hair standing nearby.

Clint walked to her and asked, "Where's the man Coltraine left behind?"

"He left. And he already took one of my girls with him, so don't try to take another."

"No, you don't understand." Clint lowered his voice and stepped even closer to her. Even though he couldn't see anyone who looked like they might be one of Coltraine's men, Clint wasn't about to get careless. "I'm a friend of Rachel's. Was she here?"

Jennifer turned and walked quickly into the next room. Clint followed her and stood so he could see both Jennifer and the hallway.

"She was here a while ago," Jennifer said.

"How long ago?"

"Less than an hour."

"What did she do?" Clint asked.

"She asked about the same man you did. I told her to leave him be, but she said she was out to put him and the rest of them down for good. I don't know how she could manage such a thing, but—"

"Where is she now? I need to find her before she does anything stupid."

Jennifer shrugged and replied, "She wanted to meet with Mr. Rice as if she were one of my own girls. I told her that might not be a good idea, but she insisted. Since she wanted to go so badly, I lent her a red dress and introduced her to him."

"And where is she now?" Clint asked, trying not to sound too impatient.

"She's gone. Both of them are."

"What? I thought you just introduced them."

"That was almost an hour ago," she explained. "She talked with him for a while, then he took her to a room. They were in there for a little bit and then he came out with her. After that, they both left."

"You said they only left about a half hour ago."

Shaking her head a bit, Jennifer said, "However she convinced him, she did it quickly. From what I've heard from other girls that have been with Mr. Rice, that's not much of a surprise." Suddenly, Jennifer pulled in a quick breath and reached out for Clint's head. "Are you hurt?"

"I'll be all right. Apparently, I got a bit more rest than I thought." Taking a watch from his pocket, Clint took one look at the time and cursed under his breath. "Damn! Do you know where they might have gone?"

"It looked like Mr. Rice was leading the way and he never really says where he goes. You might want to ask Sergeant Bray, though."

"Thanks for your help," Clint said, ignoring her other suggestion completely. When he started to turn so he could leave, he was stopped by a gentle yet insistent hand around his elbow.

"You've got to understand," Jennifer said. "Those men come here and take these girls off to . . . I don't even know where. All I do know is that they're good girls and I never hear from them again. That friend of yours said she wanted to help and she meant it. I could tell by the look in her eyes. She's the first one who ever wanted to help . . . women like us."

Clint took Jennifer's hand and told her, "She's not the only one who wants to help."

Jennifer nodded and smiled. "Head north," she said. "That's all I know about where those men go from here. They ride north and if they knew I told you that much, they'd come back and make me sorry for even lifting a finger against them."

"Don't you worry. They won't be coming back."

THIRTY-SEVEN

As much as he wanted to gather more information, find someone else who might have more to say, or even locate a track to let him know he was pointed in the right direction, north was all he had. Since it was a simple choice of using what he had or letting more time go by, Clint did the best he could with what he had.

He rode north.

As he rode Clint thought about how things had panned out since he'd started this hunt. It seemed like a year ago since he'd heard Kaylee crying at the Cherry Blossom. It seemed like weeks since he'd first met Rachel Dovetree. It seemed like a decade since he'd had a night of uninterrupted sleep.

But Clint didn't feel tired. He was fed up with running in circles and being played like a fiddle by some bastard who kidnapped women for a living. Clint might have found out plenty since he'd started after Coltraine. For one thing, he knew Coltraine was either buying working girls from their places of employment or stealing them outright. For another thing, Clint knew that these same women were probably being sold to a tribe of renegade Indians.

Clint had met plenty of Indians in his day and most of them were good folks. Like any other group of folks, however, there was bound to be some who were just plain bad. Some Indians felt entitled to take whatever they wanted from the white man, since practically everything belonging to the Indians had been stolen as well.

As much as Clint hated to admit it, that was a tough argument to fight against.

But this wasn't about striking back for land that was stolen or people who were killed. It was about money, plain and simple. Clint had found that out very early on and had only gotten it proved to him every step of the way.

Coltraine was out to make money.

All of the men riding with Coltraine were in it for money.

The assholes who handed their women over to Coltraine willingly were trying to make money or keep from losing it.

The only victims in this scheme were the women themselves. Sadly, Jennifer was right when she said that most people didn't want to lift a finger to help them. Just thinking about that made Clint see red.

Suddenly, he pulled back on his reins.

Until now, he'd been riding north and allowing Eclipse to maintain a steady gallop. Clint's mind had been wandering, simply because it seemed there wasn't much else for him to do—until he saw something that could be of some use.

And he damn near passed it by.

Clint brought Eclipse around and flicked the reins, but only let the stallion run for a few seconds before bringing him to a stop once more. Clint's eyes darted back and forth, up and down, glancing from one branch to another.

Trees were scattered on both sides of the trail and they were all full of leaves at this time of year. The sun was high in the sky, making all the colors stand out like an artist's new set of paints. Clint saw the bright green of leaves, some purple flowers, even some yellows, but he didn't stop until he saw the color he'd been looking for.

Finally, he saw red.

It wasn't at the first few trees he'd stopped at, but Clint managed to pick it out all the same. When he did, he moved Eclipse to the proper spot and leaned forward to get a better look.

"I'll be damned," he muttered as he saw the red strip of material fluttering from the branch where it had been snagged.

Standing up in his stirrups, Clint reached out to grab the material. He felt it between his fingers and figured it must have been satin or possibly a cheap blend of silk. Either choice would have been ideal to make a red dress, and a red dress was exactly what Jennifer had lent to Rachel.

Clint held the strip of material in both hands so he could examine it closely. Sure enough, there was a faint pattern on the material that sure as hell hadn't come from a flag, banner, or anything else made of satin that would have been torn out on that trail.

Even the shape of it was enough to give him hope. The edges were rough and strained, making it easy for Clint to imagine Rachel holding onto her dress tightly and ripping off that piece. Clint shook his head and looked to the north. Even though he'd somehow found the marker she'd left behind, he still wished she would have listened to him before. Her idea was insane, but by some miracle it was working.

Clint dropped down from the saddle and looked at the trail beneath his and Eclipse's feet. There were a few sets of fresh tracks, but his were the freshest and ran over the rest of them. Thinking back to what he knew about Coltraine and how he traveled, Clint guessed that Rachel must be riding with whoever had been waiting at the cathouse and nobody else.

Coltraine would have a lot more men with him, as well

as a few women. There weren't any indications that a group that big had ridden by in the last few hours. There were, however, two sets of tracks just beneath Clint's that led farther down the trail. As luck would have it, they were also headed north.

Not knowing what condition Rachel was in or if she was in any danger, Clint wasted no more time looking around at trees. He climbed onto Eclipse's back, snapped the reins and got the stallion moving again.

As much as he wanted to take off at a full run, Clint didn't want to make a wrong turn. Charging off now, knowing what he did, was the same as riding straight into a thick patch of fog that had settled in over the edge of a cliff. One lapse in judgment would take him to the end of his road. In this case, however, it would be the end of Rachel's road, as well as her sister's and Alicia Higgins's.

One thing was certain.

Clint had come too far to give up on all of them now.

THIRTY-EIGHT

Clint kept riding and strained his eyes to keep sight of the tracks he was following. The trail widened into a flat mix of rock and hardened soil that wound between trees, rocks and through a few trickling creeks. Although it was a pretty trail and pleasant to follow, it wasn't good at holding tracks.

Before long, Clint was unable to keep sight of the tracks without occasionally stopping to climb down and lead Eclipse by the reins so his eyes were closer to the ground. Soon, even that wasn't enough and Clint was nearly misled by deeper tracks that had been put down when the ground was wetter. Since there hadn't been any rain for more than week, Clint knew those deeper tracks were a hell of a lot older.

Swearing under his breath, Clint rode back to the spot where he'd last seen the tracks for certain. From there, he pieced together what he'd learned about where Coltraine and his men were headed. Crow territory was due north and the hills that he'd been told about were only slightly west of north themselves.

Clint knew all too well that sometimes a man needed to have some faith. He knew it, but that didn't mean that he had to like it every time he was forced to take a leap himself. But he was all out of options and so he kept riding.

A few miles later, he saw several branches from the trail, which led in three different directions. The branch headed east didn't seem like much of an option, but the ones headed north and west were definite possibilities. He pulled back on the reins a bit, tried to have some faith and watched for more red.

Before too long, he saw it.

Just like the last time, the red he spotted was a shred of material from a dress. Unlike the last time, this shred was tied around a stick that was large enough to keep the makeshift flag in place. That stick was lying directly beside the part of the trail that branched west, so that was the direction Clint rode.

Clint kept right on riding for a good chunk of the day. He didn't spot another shred of Rachel's dress, but he also didn't spot any parts of the trail that veered off course. The flat road continued winding its way west, before eventually veering to the north.

By the end of the day, Clint could see the hills directly in front of him. There weren't many tracks along the way, but the ones he occasionally saw might very well have been the ones he'd been following at the start of this ride.

He kept riding through the night, constantly reminding himself about the faith that was supposed to be keeping him going. Whenever he couldn't quite feel the faith, Clint passed the time by cursing Rachel for knocking him on the back of the head and taking off on her own. Every so often, he cursed himself for betting on a marginal hand back in Markton when he'd been leery of staying in that game in the first place.

All of those things took turn fueling Clint's fire until he rode through a cluster of trees and found scattered bits of a settlement on the other side. It wasn't quite a town, but it was much more than a camp. It was also composed of a mix of cabins and teepees, just like the big Indian had described it.

Clint brought Eclipse to a stop and wondered if he should trust the word of the Indian.

Now, more than ever, a bit of faith was needed.

THIRTY-NINE

Even though they'd stopped a little sooner than she'd expected, Rachel felt like she'd been on the longest ride of her life. Rice had led her on a horse from the livery instead of her own. She'd discovered the reason for that when she'd tried to steer the horse off the trail once or twice. The animal only took commands from Rice, which might have been an impressive trick if it didn't keep her from escaping.

So she'd quickly settled on her backup plan, which was also the reason she'd chosen such a brightly colored, and ill-fitting, dress. She'd torn pieces from her dress while making the occasional bit of small talk with Rice. When she'd needed to cover the sound of material being shredded, she'd whistled or complimented Rice on his riding style. When she'd tossed the markers down, she prayed all her mindless chatter would do more than stroke Rice's ego.

They arrived at the village as the sun was on its way down. Rice headed straight to one of the cabins, where he jumped from the saddle, tied off his horse and motioned for Rachel to follow.

"Looks like you tore up that dress," he said.

Rachel looked down and even seemed shocked to see the tattered remains of her skirt. "Damn."

"Don't worry about that. Donnie'll fix you up with a new one. You'll need to wear it to impress your new bosses."

"Who's Donnie?" she asked, wondering if another man could possibly be as easy to please if she was forced to prove herself again.

After tossing his saddlebags into the cabin, Rice grabbed Rachel by the wrist and dragged her toward the teepees. "Right over here."

Rachel was practically thrown into the teepee, only to find a small boy and a slender Indian woman stitching a pattern into tanned leather. Although both of the Indians were surprised by the sudden intrusion, they quickly recognized Rice's face.

"This one needs a new dress," he said. "Her name's . . . what's your name again?"

Despite the fact that she'd given him the wrong name before, Rachel couldn't help but be offended that it had already been forgotten. "Lilly. I told you my name's Lilly."

"Fine, whatever. Fix Lilly here a new dress." With that, Rice left the teepee and dropped the flap in place over the entrance.

The Indian woman's eyes wandered up and down over Rachel's body. Even though Rachel had been scrutinized more in the last few weeks than in the rest of her life combined, this time she felt comfortable. The Indian woman wasn't sizing her up the way the men had done those other times. Instead, she looked for what she needed and then reached around to take some skins from a pile behind her.

"This will not fit you," the Indian woman said while waving to the dress she'd been working on before. "I can make you another."

Rachel nodded. "Thank you."

After returning Rachel's smile with a quick one of her own, the other woman bustled about her task.

"Who's Donnie?" Rachel asked.

The woman shook her head and put on a tired smile. "The man who brought you here calls me that, even after I tell him it is not my name."

"What is your name?"

"Dyani." She looked up and saw the perplexed look on Rachel's face. "Dee-yah-nee."

After sounding it out for herself, Rachel repeated the name and brought a more genuine smile to Dyani's face. "What does it mean?"

Dyani stopped in the middle of a stitch and studied Rachel's face. "Deer."

"That's pretty."

"Your name is Lilly?"

Just then, Rachel almost corrected her. Even though Dyani seemed friendly enough, Rachel fought back her impulse and nodded.

"That is pretty, too."

The little boy in the teepee looked to be no more than five or six years old. He kept in his corner and wouldn't take his eyes off of Rachel.

"Do you see all the women that come through here?" Rachel asked.

Dyani shook her head quickly, but it seemed more out of distaste for the question than a lack of an answer. "Sometimes, there are many. I make new clothes for most of them."

Already, the leather in Dyani's hand was taking shape. It wasn't anything too fancy, but it would be a fairly good dress very soon. "You should probably not ask about the others," she said while concentrating on her stitching. "The white men here do not like that."

Rachel glanced over her shoulder at the entrance flap of the teepee. Even though it was still closed, she was well aware of how thin the hides were that made up the circular wall. "I need to know about a specific woman that could have been brought here. Her name's Emily."

Dyani kept shaking her head and stitching the leather.

"It's important that I find her." Reaching out with one hand, Rachel took hold of Dyani's arm so she couldn't make another stitch. "Are you listening to me?"

"I hear you," Dyani said. "But you would be smart not to ask such questions. The men here do not like to answer questions from the women."

"Are you here because you want to be here? Or are you being held prisoner?"

"I am here to do a job and that is what I need to do." Suddenly, Dyani's face took on a more intense quality as she stared directly into Rachel's eyes. "If you have a job, you should do it. If you do not prove yourself useful to these men, they will kill you. The ground outside this village is full of women who did not do their jobs."

"The woman I'm looking for is my sister," Rachel said. "Her name's Emily. Do you know if she was here or not?"

"All I know is that you should either please these men or run when you have the chance."

With that, Dyani shut her mouth and went back to stitching. Two seconds later, the teepee's flap was pulled aside and Rice stuck his head in.

"Come on," he grunted. "Donnie'll bring that dress over when it's done."

FORTY

Rachel was dragged from the teepee to a cabin in the middle of camp. The cabin was more like a shack and had just enough room inside for two cots, a small trunk and a washbasin.

Rice all but threw her into the shack and said, "This is just temporary. You'll have some company soon enough."

"What about my dress?" Rachel asked a little too anxiously. When she saw the look on Rice's face, she added, "This one's barely going to last after all the rips it got."

"I told you Donnie will be here. She's real quick. After that, I can come back and see how easy it is to get you out of it."

Responding to Rice's lecherous smile, Rachel nodded and sat down on the cot. As soon as he left, she got up and began searching the small room. The first thing she noticed was that the shack's door locked from the outside and didn't so much as budge when she tried opening it. Both windows were equally stubborn and weren't big enough for her to crawl through, anyhow. Before she could do much more checking, Rachel heard the latch being opened on the door.

Another man stuck his head in to get a look at her. He

was younger than Rice and hadn't shaved for at least a week. He seemed disappointed to find Rachel dressed and not lying on the bed for him. "Yer new clothes are ready."

"Good."

Dyani pushed her way past the younger man and turned around to look at him. It took some effort, but she managed to get the door shut so he was left outside.

"I can talk while we are in here," Dyani said. "These shacks are made to keep women and their screams inside, but that man will be standing right outside."

Dyani unfolded the bundle she was carrying and held it up to Rachel. The dress was similar to the simple one she, herself, was wearing and was even adorned with a few small decorations. "Put this on. I made it long and fit so that it is hard to be pulled up. Most of these men like to grab at us like we are toys."

"So you are being held here as a prisoner?" Rachel asked as she pulled off her torn red dress and took the one Dyani was offering.

"I was one of their first trades with the Crow. My husband thought I could bear no more children, so he traded me for a woman like you. One with lighter skin and golden hair."

"I'm sorry."

"The truth is that I would not bear any more children. Not to him. He was a cruel father. I am fortunate that I managed to bring my son with me."

"Did Coltraine bring the woman who you were traded for?" Rachel asked.

"Yes. It was a woman he was supposed to bring to another town, but she was giving him too much trouble. He traded her for me and tried to sell me to another tribe, but could not. They said they wanted white women and could get lots of money for them."

"The Crow are buying these women?"

Dyani shook her head. "They trade for them, but they

sell them to someone else. It is only a small group of Crow who are doing this. Nobody from my tribe."

"Is your tribe the Koko people? Someone told us that's who lived in this village."

When Dyani heard that, she crinkled her nose and shook her head. "Koko is a Blackfoot word for night. It was given to us by some of the traitors who ride with these white slavers. They follow Coltraine and call him Shadow Walker like he is one of our own. None of these men are a tribe. They have no pride and no honor. It is not brave to steal women and hide them away until they can be sold."

"Who buys them?"

"I do not know. I stay here and am not allowed to leave. I see the women come and go and the ones who aren't killed here never come back. There are dogs in every tribe, who make the rest look like dogs as well."

Rachel sighed and straightened the dress over her shoulders. "Believe me, my people have plenty of dogs among them, too."

Still fretting with the hem, Dyani said, "These dogs who think they are Crow and Shoshone are just animals. The only ones worse than them are the animals who pay to take the women that are stolen from their homes. Even if I did know who they were, it would not help. They are far from here. I can try to give you a chance to escape, but even that will be dangerous for you."

"I'm not worried about that. I need to know if you remember my sister coming through here."

"I know where to look, but there are so many that come and go. I cannot remember them all. Some don't even leave a trace."

"Anything you could do would help."

"Tell me what she looks like," Dyani said as she lowered herself to one knee and made some last-minute alterations.

"I can do better than that," Rachel replied as she reached for a locket that always hung from her neck. She opened the locket to reveal two pictures. "This is Emily," she said while pointing to one of the pictures.

"And who is the other one?"

"That's Lilly. She's my mother. My real name is Rachel. I lied about it before because I didn't want any of these bastards to know who I am."

Dyani smiled, but there wasn't a trace of humor on her face. "These men do not care who you are. All they care is if you are a woman." She stared at the picture in the locket and then nodded. "But I will see what I can find out about your sister. Like they say, though, don't hold your breath."

Rachel put the locket away and looked around to see if the door was open or if anyone was standing outside the windows. "I may be able to get us both out of here. Someone is coming for me."

"Nobody will come," Dyani said sadly. "I gave up that dream a long time ago."

"The man I'm talking about should be right on my heels. He might even be here tonight. If we can get to you, will you come away with us?"

"I will not leave my son behind."

"I don't think Clint would want to leave that boy behind, either."

Dyani tied up the stitch she'd been working on and stood up. "If your man makes it here, he will be the only one to get so far."

"Clint's just the man for the job," Rachel said confidently, even though she felt a pang of worry in the bottom of her stomach.

"If that is so, I will do everything I can to help him. I don't think there will be another who is strong enough to make it here."

There was a single knock on the door before it was pushed open. The younger man stuck his head inside and once again looked disappointed by what he saw. "You done with that dress?"

"Yes," Dyani replied.

"Then start working on more of 'em. Coltraine'll need 'em when he gets back."

Nodding once to Rachel was all Dyani needed to do in order to send one last message. That nod told Rachel to be strong and remember the things she'd been told. It also told her not to worry about Dyani holding up her own end. Once Dyani saw the nod in return, she lowered her eyes and turned toward the door.

"I'll be checkin' on you later," the young man said to Rachel as he grinned hungrily.

After that, the door was slammed shut and the latch was dropped into place.

FORTY-ONE

Rachel wasn't sure how long she sat in that shack. Sometimes, it seemed as if she'd just arrived and other times, it felt as if she'd been there for days. The light coming through the windows faded away before going out completely. Although she had yet to hear or see any sign of Clint, she also hadn't seen any of the other men who'd promised to pay her a visit.

As she waited, Rachel didn't have much else to do besides think. Since thinking only led to some dark possibilities floating through her mind, she examined her new dress instead. The stitches were perfectly spaced and uniform in size. It fit her perfectly and was a little hard to move in, but that had been by Dyani's design. Rachel smirked at the thought of someone fighting to pull that dress off of her.

Her smirk faded pretty quickly as that same thought lingered for a bit.

As if picking up on her thoughts, someone knocked on the door and lifted the latch.

Rachel's first idea was to get away from the door, even though she didn't know who was coming through. Her instinct was correct, since it was the younger man from earlier that day who stepped inside. He grinned at her and shut

164

the door behind him as Rachel climbed onto one of the cots and put her back to the wall.

"Hey there, pretty lady," the man said.

He looked hungrier than before and was already unbuckling his belt as he walked forward. He also wasn't wearing a gun, which put a crimp in Rachel's plan to find one for herself.

"The Injuns we're sellin' you to like to see you in them dresses Donnie makes. Them Mexicans like 'em, too. They say they keep your legs nice and warm."

"I thought I was going to work at a place," Rachel said. "That's what Mr. Rice told me. You'd better talk to him before you lay one finger on me."

The young man just kept stalking forward. "I already had a word with him," he said. "And he told me you were a fine piece of pussy. You ain't the first one to come through here, just so's you know."

Pulling his pants down and climbing onto the cot, he added, "And you also better know what happens to the bitches who don't do what they're told. We can make you pray for whatever it is them Mexicans do to you once they get your pretty ass south of the border."

Rachel gritted her teeth and started swinging at the young man as he crawled toward her. Even as her fists landed and her nails drew blood, all she did was widen the smile on the young man's face.

That smile even stayed there as the door behind him was pushed open and heavy steps thumped against the floor. The young man kept his eyes glued to Rachel and even managed to grab hold of her leg before he was hauled off the cot and tossed onto the other one.

"Are you all right?" Clint asked.

For a moment, Rachel couldn't believe her eyes. All she did was nod and then Clint was lunging toward the second cot. She looked over to the door and saw Dyani there, closing it quietly and standing there to make sure it stayed shut.

"Who the hell are you?" the young man asked.

Clint didn't say a word. Instead, he grabbed the man by the front of his shirt and slammed his fist directly into the man's nose. There was a dull crunching sound, followed by another as Clint delivered a second punch to the same spot.

That second punch to his already broken nose was too much for the younger man. His eyes turned glassy and then rolled up into his head as he went slack.

Clint dropped him onto the cot and took a quick look out the nearest window. "Looks like we've still got some time," he said. "Are you hurt, Rachel?"

To answer that, Rachel rushed forward and wrapped her arms around Clint's neck. She peppered his face with kisses and then kissed him deeply on the mouth.

As much as he hated to do it, Clint pulled her away and said, "I'll take that as a yes. What in the hell possessed you to take off on your own like that?"

"It worked, didn't it?" she asked breathlessly.

"I'm surprised you're still alive."

"These assholes don't kill women. They trade them."

"They kill plenty," Clint said. "I've seen their graves."

"What?"

"On my way into this camp. They're buried in the woods a stone's throw from here, marked by Crow symbols. That's where I found Dyani."

The Indian woman nodded. "I was there checking for your sister."

"What . . . what do you mean?" Rachel asked.

"I bury them because these men would dump them. I mark their graves with my people's holy symbols as well as things that would have belonged to them. Here," she said while holding out a small pouch, "look and see if any of these were your sister's."

Rachel held the pouch in one hand and looked to Clint.

"Go on," he told her. "I don't think anyone saw us coming in, but they'll miss Dyani before too long."

Rachel took the pouch and slowly shook its contents onto the cot. Trinkets of all shapes and sizes fell onto the rough blanket. Some were bits of jewelry, while others were pieces of photographs or even marbles and business cards. Seeing all those personal effects brought a sadness to Rachel's heart that felt like a weight. That weight became even heavier when she saw a locket similar to her own drop from the pouch.

"Oh, my God." She sighed.

Rachel opened the locket and immediately turned pale. Her fingers tightened around it and tears streamed down her face.

"I'm sorry," Dyani said.

Clint rubbed Rachel's back and told her, "You can stay here and wait for me. I've got an idea."

"No," Rachel said vehemently. "Whatever you're doing to hurt these men, I want to be a part of it."

FORTY-TWO

Two men stood outside one of the nearby cabins and smoked their cigarettes. They laughed and joked to one another while tossing the occasional comment toward the row of smaller cabins with the latches on the outside of the doors.

"Come on Stewie," one of the men shouted. "If you can't get yer pecker hard by now, it ain't gonna happen!"

Both men laughed at that, while looking around to see if they had an appreciative audience. Although there were a few Indians sitting at their teepees, they were either women or children, neither of which thought the joke was very funny. The rest of the men in the camp were scattered among the other cabins and weren't standing around outside.

"Stewwwie!" the second man hollered, as if he were calling a pig. "Save some of that bitch for us, boy!"

When they still didn't get a response, both of them fixed their eyes on the cabin where Rachel was being held.

"How long's he been in there?"

"He said he was goin' in about fifteen minutes ago, I think. We've only been standing out here for five."

The first man turned so one ear was pointed at the cabin. "You even hear anything comin' from in there?"

"No," the other replied as he flicked his cigarette to the ground. "Let's go have us a look."

Both of them had their hands resting upon their holstered guns as they walked toward Rachel's shack. Their eyes were fixed on the door of the shack as they walked straight past a pair of outhouses. Clint watched both of the men walk by as he stood with his back pressed against the closest of those two outhouses.

As soon as the men walked past him, Clint lunged forward to grab hold of their collars. Using a burst of strength, he pulled and jerked the men off balance, then dragged them straight down so they lost their footing completely.

Both of them landed with a heavy thump and scrambled around to get a look at who'd ambushed them. Clint got to the bigger of the two men before he could do much of anything and knocked him out with a swift kick to the chin.

The remaining man on the ground went for his gun, but got Clint's fist in his face before he could clear leather. The punch started behind Clint's head, traveled all the way down and landed like a rock to drop the man flat onto his back. Even before he emptied his lungs with a surprised gasp, the man was being dragged into the cabin next to Rachel's.

"Do you know where to find some rope?" Clint asked.

Dyani nodded. "I will get it."

As the Indian woman left, Rachel stepped into the empty cabin. She took the gun from the unconscious man's holster and pointed it at him until Clint dragged the first one in as well. Even though both men were obviously out for the time being, she was tempted to pull her trigger.

"I'm sorry about your sister," Clint said.

She looked over to him and lowered the gun.

Clint kept watch for anyone else moving around the camp, but turned to check on Rachel. "Are you going to be all right? If you don't want to do this . . ."

"I told you already that I want to keep going. I'll be fine.

There's going to be other women who need help. Just because I was too late to save Emily doesn't mean I can't be of some use to someone else."

Turning his back to the door, Clint walked over to her and held her by the shoulders. "I won't hear one more bit of that talk," he snarled. "You've done nothing but help since the first time I crossed your path. I haven't known you for long, but I've rarely met someone who was so hell-bent on their purpose. I've got a nasty scar on the back of my head to prove as much."

"Sorry about that," Rachel said with a wince.

"You did it to help your sister. I may not agree with it, but I'll give you hell for it later. Right now, you got me here and I even got here before most of the rest of Coltraine's gang, so we've still got a chance to pull this off. I need to know if you're strong enough to see this through to the end, though."

Rachel had tears in her eyes, but the strength behind them was undeniable. "I was strong enough to put you on your ass, wasn't I?"

Clint laughed and nodded. "Yeah, you were. Now, I got a look around this place before I ran into Dyani and there's only five armed men and about twice that many Indians. The only Indians I saw were women and children and Dyani says they won't lift a finger to help the others if push comes to shove. There's only three armed men left, but there's no telling how much time we have before Coltraine and the rest of his gang get here."

"So I guess we need to get busy."

"You're right again."

FORTY-THREE

Clint just happened to catch one of the three armed men left in camp as he was walking around a corner to check on his two compadres. Clint's arm smashed into the gunman's face, knocking him out before he hit the ground.

Another one was in the same spot that he'd been in when Clint had first arrived at camp: sleeping in one of the cabins next to the teepees. That man started to wake up at the sound of creaking boards. When he opened his eyes to see if anyone had walked into his cabin, he was just in time to see Clint staring back at him from the shadows.

Clint aimed his fist at the man's chin, but only hit a pillow after the man rolled to one side. The cabin wasn't much bigger than the shack where Rachel had been locked in, but it was big enough for the man to have some room to move once he was off his bed. The man's holster was around his waist and he went for his gun without hesitation.

Clint drew and fired his modified Colt before the other man could blink. His shot drilled a hole through the center of the man's chest and threw him back against a wall. The man landed hard enough to shake the cabin and then slid down into a seated position. His eyes were blank, but his final twitch caused his finger to tighten around the trigger of his gun.

The shot sounded like a cannon had been fired, mainly because Clint had been hoping to keep things quiet. He knew there were still others in the camp and he didn't want to bet that most of them were on his side.

"Are you all right?" Rachel asked as she rushed to the cabin's doorway.

Clint wheeled around to aim at her out of pure reflex, but he lowered his gun as soon as he recognized Rachel's face. "This one's dead."

"And Dyani is tying up the man you left outside. That means Rice is still around here."

"Who?"

"The man who brought me here from Fort Marsden. He's still around here somewhere."

"Rachel, get down!" Clint shouted.

Before she could move, she felt a gun barrel poking into her back.

"No, you'd best stay put," Rice said from behind her.

Clint had seen the man approaching her, but only after it was too late to do anything about it.

Standing with Rachel as a shield, Rice looked over her shoulder and even took a moment to smell her hair. "Drop that pistol," he demanded.

Clint lowered the gun slowly. "Anything you say."

The instant he felt the end of his barrel touch the top of his holster, Clint snapped the Colt back up and fired a shot. He didn't have to look down the barrel. All he did was point his finger where he wanted the shot to go and years of practice took care of the rest.

That shot blazed a path through Rice's skull and left a vacant yet surprised look on his face. His arm hung to his side and then Rice's finger clenched on his trigger to send his final shot into the floor.

"Serves you right, you dirty prick," Rachel said as she turned around and shoved him over. "I just wish I could've fired that shot myself."

"We don't have time to make wishes," Clint said. "We need to hurry up and get this place looking like it used to before the rest of those men get here. I got ahead of them, but it couldn't have been by too much."

As he walked outside, Clint looked around to see if anyone else was on the way to stand against him. What he found was enough to make him wonder if he hadn't misjudged his situation in a big way.

Outside the cabin, every Indian in the camp was lined up and staring straight at him. Clint felt his hand clench around his pistol, but he knew he wouldn't be able to take all of them if they decided to move at once.

The strange thing about them was that the Indians stared at him calmly. Even the children looked as if they were simply watching the sun rise. Just looking at them was enough to make Clint feel a bit calmer himself.

"You folks might want to find someplace to hide," Clint said.

One of the Indians stepped forward. He was an old man with a stooped back and silver hair that hung almost to his waist in two neat braids. "We want to help," he said.

"You can help by making sure you're out of the line of fire."

"That will be done, but that will not be all you need us to do. You do not have time to argue with me," the old man added. "I will not sit and hide when the chance we have been waiting for has finally arrived."

"All right then. The first thing I need is for this place to look just the way Coltraine is expecting it to look."

"And then what?"

Clint had to smile at the old man's determination to deal himself into this hand. "How many guns do you think you can scrounge up?"

Now, it was the old man's turn to smile.

FORTY-FOUR

The old Indian was right. They didn't have a moment to spare before the rumble of horses could be heard approaching the small village. Even so, there had been more than enough time for the unconscious gunmen to be tied up, stripped of their weapons and dumped into the same shack that Rachel had been kept in when she'd first arrived.

By the time Coltraine and his men rode into the village, they found it to be just as sleepy as when they'd left it. There was one small difference however. This time, Clint Adams stood in the middle of the village waiting for them. He had his rifle propped on his left shoulder and his right hand hanging loosely at his side.

Coltraine rode forward and signaled for the others to stop. He flipped his hat off so it hung around his neck and revealed his full head of curly, dark hair. Nine horses were clustered around and behind him. Three of those were ridden by dirty-faced gunmen. Two were ridden by Indians and four had women riding sidesaddle with their ankles bound and their wrists tied to their saddle horns by a thick knot of rope.

"Who the hell might you be?" Coltraine asked.

"I'm the one who'll be escorting these good folks back to their homes," Clint said.

Coltraine smiled and looked around. As he did so, his gunmen and the Indians moved forward to form a firing line.

"We're all good folks, mister," Coltraine said. "And this here's our home. You must be mistaken."

Clint shook his head. "No mistake."

Narrowing his eyes, Coltraine studied Clint carefully as if he didn't quite know what to make of him. Finally, he looked over to his right where a gunman with a scruffy beard was leaning forward in his saddle to get a better look for himself.

"Anyone know who the fuck this is?" Coltraine asked.

The bearded gunman shook his head. "Probably just some bounty hunter."

"Or maybe he knows one of our lady friends," another gunman offered. This one was younger and had close-cropped hair that was so blond that it looked more like peach fuzz sprouting from his scalp.

"He was at Fort Marsden," one of the two Indians said. His face and chest were both painted with a jagged design that looked like a combination of animal claws and shards of broken glass.

"You sure about that?" Coltraine asked.

The painted Indian nodded. "I saw his face there."

That seemed to be enough for Coltraine, because he shrugged and looked back to Clint. "So you were at the fort and decided to see what kind of business proposal I was offering to the girls I collected?"

"You heard me the first time. I came to escort them home." As he spoke, Clint made sure to speak slowly and not to say anything to spark a fight right away. He mainly wanted to draw Coltraine's attention as well as his men away from the women who were tied to the horses behind them.

Clint couldn't see much of Rachel, apart from a shadow

moving behind the group and toward the horses at the rear. As he'd been talking, Clint could see her shadowy figure moving to each of the captive women and helping them down. No matter how many times he'd seen how well Rachel could move without making a sound, it was still impressive to see her in action.

"You men can ride away and never come back," Clint said. "I'll give you that chance. But you're leaving the women and the rest of these people to go where they please."

Coltraine sat up and put his hand on his gun. When he did, he saw Clint do the same. When he stopped, Clint stopped. Keeping his hand in place, Coltraine said, "These Injuns can go wherever they damn well please!"

"We're captives!" the old Indian shouted from one of the nearby teepees. He stepped forward with a rifle in his hands. "Captives forced to stay here to clean your clothes, cook your food and help hide the other captives you bring back. Not anymore."

"Fine," Coltraine grunted. "Have it your own damn way. Kill this prick!"

The gunmen to Coltraine's right and left both went for their guns. Clint drew his Colt and fired in one fluid motion to blast one of the gunmen from his saddle. He fired again to hit the man while he was still falling, so the gunman was dead before his back touched the ground.

The bearded gunman managed to clear leather, but was caught in the side by a shot from the old Indian's rifle. He gritted his teeth and fired a quick shot toward the Indian, but only managed to blow a hole through the teepee.

Clint was about to finish the bearded gunman when he saw one of the Indians on horseback raise a rifle to his shoulder. Reflexively dropping to one knee, Clint aimed at the Indian and pulled his trigger.

There was a spray of blood as the Indian fell from his saddle and landed in a heap. Holding a bloody hand to his

neck, the Indian scrambled to his feet as the other painted
Indian dropped from his own horse to join him.

From one of the other teepees, an Indian woman started
firing one of the guns taken from the men who were currently tied up and locked away in a cabin. She and two
other women unleashed a barrage of lead, which not only
hit the Indian with the wounded neck but also took out the
gunman who was moving up to Coltraine's side.

The surviving painted Indian landed with both feet
squarely on the ground, took a tomahawk from his belt and
fearlessly charged Clint.

Clint fired one shot, but missed because he'd been
forced to rush after shifting his aim. He fired again and
caught the painted Indian in the ribs, but that still wasn't
enough to stop him.

Before Clint could fire again, the tomahawk was cutting
through the air and coming straight toward his head. He
rolled to one side and heard the tomahawk slice through
the air before thumping into the dirt less than a foot away
from him.

When Clint righted himself, he saw Coltraine aiming a
pistol directly at him.

The painted Indian had already retrieved his tomahawk
and was snarling as he prepared to swing again.

Clint held his ground, watched Coltraine's eyes and
then jumped aside the instant he knew Coltraine was going
to pull his trigger.

Coltraine's gun barked once. His round hissed through
the air, missed its target by less than an inch and punched a
hole through the chest of the painted Indian who was about
to attack Clint from behind.

The painted Indian stood dazed for a moment and then
dropped over.

Clint stood up and saw a similar dazed look on Coltraine's
face.

Suddenly, Coltraine pointed his gun at the Indian women. "I'm gonna shoot these bitches and it'll be your fault!"

"Go ahead and try," Clint said.

Coltraine backed his horse up while keeping his gun aimed at them. "You think I won't? You'd better let me go or these women will die!"

Clint shrugged, but didn't lower his gun.

While bringing his horse around, Coltraine turned to take aim at the closest prisoner he had. All he found was a bunch of horses wearing empty saddles and one woman standing to the side.

Rachel had a gun in her hand and a smile on her face as she took aim. She kept that smile on her face as she pulled the trigger and blew a hole through Coltraine's heart.

FORTY-FIVE

The Indian women and children were busy tending to the captive women and seeing to any wounds they had. Clint walked from teepee to teepee to make sure the women were all right. He also asked each of them one question.

"What's your name?"

He didn't get the answer he wanted until he got to the next to last woman to be released.

"Alicia," she said.

Clint bent down to eye level and studied the woman who sat nursing her bloodied wrists. "Do you have a sister?" he asked.

She nodded weakly. "Yes. Her name's Kaylee."

"I'm riding back to Markton," he said with a smile. "Perhaps you'd like to come along with me?"

The woman stared at him as if she wasn't sure she'd truly heard him say those words. When she saw him nod, she lunged at him and wrapped both arms tightly around Clint's neck. "Oh, thank you," she said in a breathless rush. "Thank you, thank you, thank you, thank you."

Rachel watched from the side, but couldn't watch for very long before leaving.

Once Clint was able to break free from Alicia's grasp,

he went outside to find Rachel standing at the edge of the village.

"I think there's going to be other women wanting to come with us," Clint said.

"After the show you put on, I wouldn't be surprised if all of them wanted you to escort them."

"And they might also like it if you came along. After all, they haven't had very good luck with men lately."

Rachel hung her head and laughed. "I don't know. The ride shouldn't be anything you can't handle."

"It might do you some good, too. Your sister may be gone, but a lot of these women aren't much more than frightened girls. They could use a sister right about now, too."

Looking up, Rachel nodded. "That sounds nice."

"Good. We can leave in the morning. Actually, we'll *have* to leave in the morning," Clint added. "The Indians are planning on packing up their camp and burning the cabins down to the ground."

"Yeah," Rachel said. "Dyani told me Shadow Walker cursed this land."

With that, she grabbed Clint's hand and pulled him behind her as she walked away from the village.

"What are you doing?" he asked as she led him to a little spot near a small, trickling river.

Rachel pushed him down and stood over him while unbuttoning her shirt. "I never got a chance to make up for hitting you on the head."

"You don't have to make up for anything," Clint said. "In fact, you did a better job than I—"

"I know I don't have to do anything," she whispered.

When Clint saw her unbuckle her belt and slide her pants over her hips, he quickly did the same. As soon as he kicked off his jeans, Rachel was straddling him and lowering herself down. The smooth skin of her thighs brushed against Clint's hips and she used one hand to stroke his cock to a full erection.

"This," she whispered while guiding him into her, "is because I want to."

Clint let out a sigh as he felt her wet lips slide all the way down the length of his penis. When he was fully inside of her, she leaned down so her hair brushed his face and her breath could be felt against his neck and ear. Clint wrapped his arms around her and held her tightly. When his hands drifted to cup her tight backside, he could feel her start to rock gently back and forth.

After she'd ridden him for a few quiet minutes, Clint rolled her onto her back and buried himself inside of her again. Rachel let out a satisfied breath, smiled broadly and wrapped her legs around him.

"You look like you've been thinking about this for a while," Clint said.

In fact, Rachel was thinking about the performance she'd put on with Rice and how pathetic it was that Rice had responded to it. "Actually, I'm just glad to know there's still at least one man in this world who knows how to treat a woman."

Watch for

THE SAPPHIRE GUN

305th novel in the exciting GUNSMITH series
from Jove

Coming in May!

Giant Westerns featuring The Gunsmith

GIANT-SIZED ADVENTURE FROM AVENGING ANGEL LONGARM.

LONGARM AND THE OUTLAW EMPRESS
0-515-14235-2

WHEN DEPUTY U.S. MARSHAL CUSTIS LONG STOPS A STAGECOACH ROBBERY, HE TRACKS THE BANDITS TO A TOWN CALLED ZAMORA. A HAVEN FOR THE LAWLESS, IT'S RULED BY ONE OF THE MOST POWERFUL, BRILLIANT, AND BEAUTIFUL WOMEN IN THE WEST...A WOMAN WHOM LONGARM WILL HAVE TO FACE, UP CLOSE AND PERSONAL.

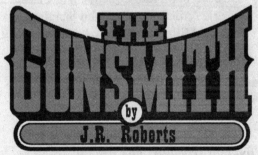